D1525731

SHAG CARPET ACTION

SHAG CARPET ACTION

STORIES BY MATTHEW FIRTH

ANVIL PRESS | VANCOUVER | 2011

LIBRARY AND ARCHIVES CANADA CATALOGUING IN PUBLICATION

Firth, Matthew, 1965-

    Shag carpet action : stories / Matthew Firth.

ISBN: 978-1-897535-84-4

    I. Title.

PS8561.I66S53 2011   C813'.54   C2011-906144-9

Printed and bound in Canada.
Book design and illustrations by Ryan Lawrie

Represented in Canada by the Literary Press Group
Distributed by the University of Toronto Press

 Canada Council   Conseil des Arts   BRITISH COLUMBIA   Canadian   Patrimoine
for the Arts   du Canada   ARTS COUNCIL   Heritage   canadien
                                        An agency of the Province of British Columbia

The publisher gratefully acknowledges the financial assistance of the Canada Council for
the Arts, the Canada Book Fund, and the Province of British Columbia through the B.C.
Arts Council and the Book Publishing Tax Credit.

Anvil Press Publishers Inc.
P.O. Box 3008, Main Post Office
Vancouver, B.C. V6B 3X5 Canada
www.anvilpress.com

For Andrea, always.

ACKNOWLEDGEMENTS:

Thank you Brian Kaufman, Bill Brown, and Zsolt Alapi. Big thank you to Andrea, Samuel and Willem.

Earlier versions of some stories have appeared in *The Loose Canon, Pilot, The Veg, The Puritan* and in French translation in the anthology *Le Livres des Felures*.

CONTENTS

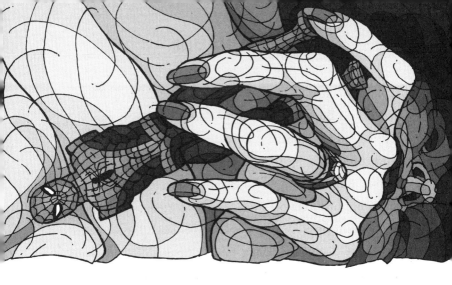

ACTION

She masturbates with an action figure—a Spider-Man about eight inches long, missing its arms. She rubs Spidey's face into her clit, up and down her labia, and then pushes him in, right up to his ankles. She gives the small, hard plastic figure more action than it bargained for.

I imagine Spider-Man's reaction inside his small, hard plastic head. I imagine being that size—having my entire face mashed into a woman's clit. Then being pushed up a woman's cunt, not able to breathe, enveloped completely by her warmth. I am not a small, hard plastic action figure, so that would have to be one huge, motherfucking giant of a woman. Bigger than a dinosaur, a blue whale even. She'd be as tall as a redwood tree. Her vagina would be the size of the front door to my house. I could get lost in there.

The masturbating woman is my neighbour, Tatiana. Yes, this is her real name. It is not a made-up, Eastern European YouPorn name. It's her real name, at least as far as I know. I have spoken with her often. She is Russian or Estonian, but she is also a typical, suburban mother and wife. Tatiana has three children: Ainsley, Ashley, and Boris. I wonder about Boris, the younger one, why Tatiana and her husband Alex reverted to their heritage for his name. Boris is the Spider-Man fanatic. He has come to my door dressed as Spider-Man three Halloweens in a row. I've seen him in warmer months racing around in a Spidey T-shirt on a Spidey tricycle, sometimes wearing a Spider-Man mask. I've seen Boris in front of their house, flipping through Spider-Man comics and books, surrounded by action figures and accessories. I have no doubt he has all the DVDs, maybe copies of the old TV show as well. He loves Spider-Man, clearly. But when he is away at grade one in the school around the corner on a quiet Tuesday morning, it's his mother, Tatiana, who really shows Spidey some good loving.

I know all this because I live across the street. The neighbourhood is young. The trees are not much more than saplings. The windows on the houses are wide and large. And with the sun in the east behind her house, at ten in the morning from my house to the west, I can see right into my neighbour's house, so well that I can see Tatiana lying on her son's bed slowly fucking herself with an action figure. Moments like this you never expect, but they happen; they really do. Pay enough attention and you will see things like this. Never mind satellite imagery and telescopic intrusions— all you really need is a pair of discreet binoculars and you can see amazing things. Yes, ninety-nine per cent of the time you witness the banal—a woman folding laundry, a man drying dishes, a little girl reading a book, a young boy playing with action figures—but once in a while you will see a beautiful Eastern European mother getting herself off in the mid-morning light.

ACTION

Tatiana is having an orgasm. Through my binoculars I see her face go purple, see the muscles at the base of her neck flex, see her pelvis jar with the impact of climax. Spider-Man is in deep, really deep. He's probably dying in there, suffocating. Or does he love it? Afterward, does he lecture the other action figures—Spider-Men with arms, Supermen, Hulks, Batmen, plus all the knights, kings, and dragons, and say something like:

"You are all virgins. You really are. You may have fucked Catwoman or some pathetic plastic princess, but they are six inches tall and made of hard plastic. You have not fucked Boris's mother. She is a giant; her vagina is massive, beyond your dreams. Yes, you've seen her in clothes. You've maybe seen her in the shower when Boris leaves you there after his bath. You've maybe strained your small, hard plastic heads to see her soap herself, wash her ass and tits, but you've never—NEVER—been anywhere near where I have been. Keep your silly arms. I don't care if Boris broke me a year ago, tore my arms off and threw them down the cold air return. I crawled away and survived. I have a new purpose now. I am his mother's special lover and the rest of you are jealous children. You are nothing but silly, silly toys."

The armless Spider-Man is king of the toy bin.

But then I wonder why Tatiana doesn't just buy a dildo, a vibrator—some kind of proper sex toy to get off. Alex? Maybe her husband Alex would object. So she fucks an eight-inch Spider-Man while her children are at school, while her husband is at work.

She is finished and I have lost interest in her. I am more interested in myself now. I think about *my* husband. I think about hard plastic, my binoculars.

I am older than Tatiana. Two of my kids are in high school, the other away at university. My husband is overweight and does not talk. He putters around the house. He loves me but he doesn't *love* me, doesn't show me any action.

I am a forty-eight-year-old woman. I might soon lose all interest in sex. It might be over for me, the sex. I will have nothing but memories, bad memories. I will stop fantasizing. I might.

For now, it's Tuesday, a quiet Tuesday. My neighbour has stopped masturbating with her Spider-Man. I think about other women. I want some change. I want something to change in my life, anything. I think about how I want to try sex with another woman. Maybe Tatiana. She has something going on, why can't I?

I think about giant vaginas. Then I think about a bed covered in warm, soft baked beans. Champagne bottles. Squirming masses of rancid-smelling maggots. The rough feel of abrasions and scar tissue under my fingers. Skull tattoos. Blood covering my lower half. My stupid husband's head on a stake, as if it's the fourteenth century and his impaled head is a warning to others. I want to warn others. I want to challenge them. I want a hundred men—a hundred of the king's best men—to line up and fuck me in the ass, one after the other. Afterward, I will stand, walk away, and pretend there was nothing to it. They will make me queen. That, or execute me in the village square. Either way, it will be change, a little action.

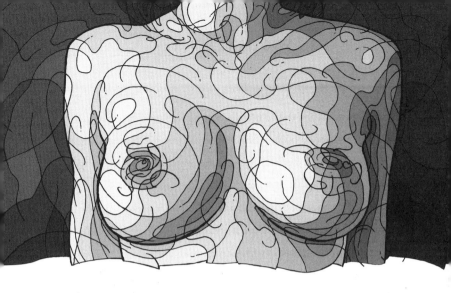

SHAG CARPET

She had hair on her tits. I was drunk but there was no mistaking it. Three or four thick hairs on the areola of each nipple. She was not shy. She was also drunk. Caroline Walters. I barely knew her. I had never spoken to her before that night. I was a grade ahead of her at school. She was in the same grade as the party's host.

I went with three other guys from grade eleven. Our intentions were simple: make out with girls younger than us, using our seniority to our advantage. It worked. I was there an hour and was going at it with Marilyn Karpeki, a pudgy girl who wore her hair in blond ringlets. I had her outside in the backyard. She balked when I tried to put a hand down her pants. She wouldn't touch my cock. I lied and said I had to go inside to pee. I lied again when I told her I'd be right back. I left Marilyn sitting on the lip of a child's sandbox.

Caroline was different. Twenty minutes after abandoning Marilyn, I hooked up with Caroline in the kitchen. We drank vodka and orange juice. We laughed and touched each other. Then

13

I took her upstairs into someone's bedroom. Jackets were piled on the bed, so we stood in the middle of the room, our hands all over each other's clothed bodies. She helped me into her pants, opened her shirt and undid her bra. She directed my hands to her strangely hairy tits. I looked at them, touched the coarse hair. Caroline moaned, then took out my cock and pulled on it, jerked me off. It didn't take long. I ejaculated on the orange shag carpet. She looked down and smiled, pleased with herself, then tucked her tits away and zipped up her pants.

"What do you think of me now?" Caroline asked.

I knew why she asked. She thought herself something of a geek, a square girl. She had a dull exterior, but obviously—when plied—was capable of more. I had no answer for her, not then. Instead, I put my face in her hair that hung down to her shoulders, pulled her close for a few seconds, then turned and went back to the party.

In my head, later, stumbling home, I came up with an answer. It was the sort of thought that came to me too late to be useful. Although, in this case, I doubted I would have had the heart to tell her. I thought: "Caroline Walters, you definitely have a future, but you really need to lose the hair on your tits first."

ASPHALT

"De Paulo, Donatelli, Scarpetti, Milenetti, Falcone, Difalco —Cement."

"McConnell, Perkins, Liebert—Saw."

"Horton, Hong, Reece, Lowsanski, Bauer, Baillgeron, Dionetti, Lewis—Weeds."

"Smitherman, Dooley, Kurtz, Sawicki—Hot box."

"Johnson, Wisner—Yardmen."

"Bickles—Elephant."

"Hamm, De Carlo, Firth—Asphalt."

We have our orders. Rosetti—the job foreman—looks us over to make sure no one has a beef with him. Then he fucks off back to his office.

Hamm stands two tables over. He grabs his lunch pail, gloves, and grunts in my direction. De Carlo is over by the water fountain. I take my knapsack and follow Hamm and the rest of the men out of the lunchroom, into the yard.

De Carlo never says much. When we get to the truck, he

opens the door and holds it for me. I sit in the middle. I always sit in the middle. I am the junior man. De Carlo wants the window so he gets it, even though the fucker is about six inches shorter than me and I could use the extra legroom. Hamm stinks like an abattoir and I hate being jammed in next to him. I hate having to listen to his chatter in my left ear.

I climb in and open Hamm's *Toronto Sun*. I flip to the sports. I check the box scores but it's mostly baseball this time of year. I don't like baseball. I take a glimpse at the Sunshine Girl. It says she likes ultimate Frisbee and big dogs. She's a brunette with nice round tits. They look real. I put the paper back on the dash.

De Carlo and I wait in silence for Hamm. He finishes his circle check and then gets in.

"Morning, gentlemen."

De Carlo mutters something. Hamm gears up. The trailer holding the BOMAG lurches behind us and we pull out of the yard.

"You got-ah the job sheet?" De Carlo says.

Hamm hands it to him.

De Carlo looks it over. He doesn't say anything. He hardly ever says anything. I've asked before to see the job sheet but Hamm and DeCarlo keep it to themselves. I don't know why. I'll find out where we're going eventually, once we get there. It's their source of power or something.

Ten minutes later Hamm stops the truck. I stay where I am. I know what's happening now. He's dropping the trailer at the job. They'll mark it with cones, check that the road cut is barricaded and then we'll go for asphalt.

De Carlo gets out to give him a hand.

ASPHALT

After, it means I'll sit in the truck cab, in the middle of these two men, for the next hour. I wish I had something to read. There were porn mags all over the floor of the cab at one time. Then De Carlo got annoyed and threw them out the window while the truck was driving down the escarpment. Hamm called him a jackass but there was nothing we could do about it.

I could use a porn mag now. I don't want to go back to the *Toronto Sun*. There's nothing in that stupid newspaper that's any use to anyone, once you've eyeballed the Sunshine Girl and checked the box scores. Then I think about the weather. I could check the weather. It's hot. It's been hot for too long and it's still only June. I check the paper and it says it's going to stay hot all week, with the chance of afternoon thunderstorms. That's not news. I throw the paper on the floor of the cab. De Carlo looks at it for a second. Then he looks at me. Then he goes back to looking out the window. Hamm just drives and whistles.

I'm bored out of my mind. I try to sleep but it goes nowhere. I go back to the *Toronto Sun*. I look at the Sunshine Girl again. The stuff about Frisbee and big dogs angers me. I don't believe it for a second. She looks intelligent. I bet she told them she likes James Joyce and Dostoevsky and they changed it, dumbed her down. I wish I had some Dostoevsky handy, or at least Bukowski.

I look back at the Sunshine Girl—Anastasia; that part could be true, her name. I toss her back on the dash and fidget in my seat. I can't take it.

"Hamm, let me out here. At the next corner. I don't want to go get asphalt. Pick me up on the way back."

There's a coffee shop on the corner.

"Your call."

De Carlo says nothing.

"Pick you up in half an hour. Stay where the fucking bosses can't see you at least."

"Yeah, no problem."

Hamm stops the truck. De Carlo slowly gets out to let me go. I feel like I'm being turned loose from prison.

De Carlo's silence really starts to piss me off after a while. He has this weird arrogance about him, like he can't be bothered to speak to mangia-cakes or something. Fuck him.

I head to the coffee shop. I order a coffee and sit at the counter. The same damned *Toronto Sun* is there, several copies. That's all there is to read. No *Hamilton Spectator*, *Globe and Mail*, no magazines, and definitely no Dostoevsky or Bukowski.

I sip my coffee. This old guy comes and sits beside me. He looks me over.

"You work for the city?"

I know where this is going.

"Yeah."

"What do you do?"

"Road work."

"What kind? I used to work construction. Cement? Sewers?"

"Asphalt. Small jobs. From road cuts. Patches and shit."

He looks me over again.

"You don't look old enough."

"I'm old enough."

"You also don't look very busy."

"Coffee." I point at my cup, half empty.

"It's eight o'clock in the morning. Coffee break already? What time did you start?"

This is what I thought. I sigh.

"Yeah, I'm on break. We started early. *Really* early."

"Where's your crew? Your truck? You take a coffee break all alone?"

I wonder why this fucker thinks he has the right.

"My crew went somewhere else. They don't like this coffee shop. Too many interruptions or something. Shitty coffee."

I stare at him. He's unruffled. He edges closer to me. Here it comes.

"I pay my taxes, son. Which means I pay your salary. And I think you're full of it. I think you're dogging it."

I look at him.

"Dogging it or Dostoevskying it?"

Now he's really pissed off. He goes, "You said asphalt, eh? Never mind asphalt. I could get your *ass fired* with one phone call."

I pick up my cup and finish the cold dregs. I reach into my pants pocket. "Here's a quarter. Knock yourself out."

I stand and head to the door. I push through the glass doors back into the blistering heat. I press my face against the window for a second, looking back at the old guy. It freaks him out just enough. He shakes his head and turns away.

Now I need somewhere else to hide. In my orange fluorescent т-shirt I can't just sit on someone's lawn and fall asleep. I can't just sit on a park bench and whistle at pretty girls walking by on their way to their office jobs. I'm a marked man, a target. Too many old shits around with nothing better to do than stick their noses in where they don't belong.

I go to a service station.

"Can I use your can?"

The guy in the John Deere cap behind the counter looks up from the Sunshine Girl. He takes me in, assesses what he sees.

"You working nearby?"

"Sort of."

"Don't make it a habit. Don't bring your whole crew round here to shit."

"You don't have to worry about that. You got my word." I hold my hands up like I'm surrendering.

He points to a key on a hook.

"Don't mess it up."

I feel like an urchin. I mean, I work for the city, but this guy in the threadbare John Deere cap seems to think I don't know how to shit in a toilet properly. It's not good when grease monkeys look down their snouts at you. Stupid, half-simian asshole.

"I won't mess up your washroom."

He grunts and goes back to ogling Anastasia.

"You ever read Dostoevsky?" I ask him as I pass.

"Hunh?"

"Forget about it."

I take a shit, wipe my ass, and leave the soiled toilet paper on the floor and on the edge of the sink. Then I wash my hands. I really scrub them. I return the key. I hold my hands up to the guy's face, so he can smell how fragrant they are.

"Good enough for you?"

He recoils.

"Get outa my garage!"

"Right. See ya, chief." I salute and walk away.

Hamm should be back any minute. I walk to the corner and try to find a bit of shade under a withering tree. The heat is too much. By two o'clock this afternoon I'll be cooked. You could serve me for dinner with potatoes on the side.

Hamm shows up. De Carlo gets out slowly. I sit in the middle. I can smell the fresh asphalt and feel the heat pressing from the back of the truck.

Hamm goes, "You keep outa trouble?"

"Always, boss."

De Carlo snorts and looks out the window.

Ten minutes later we're back at the trailer. De Carlo and I get out of the truck, take care of the cones around the trailer and take down the barricade around the hole in the road we have to patch. Hamm backs up the truck. De Carlo starts the BOMAG. I grab the oil bucket and brush. I stand there like an idiot, an imbecile with my rudimentary tools. Hamm comes around and checks whether the back bucket of the truck is aligned with the hole.

"Fuck," he says. He glares at me. "Back me up a bit for fuck sakes. Make yourself useful."

I drop the bucket and the brush. I stand where Hamm can see me in the side mirror. He's got this stupid look on his face, this semi-unbelieving look like I'm going to fuck him around, like I'm incapable of backing the truck up two feet so it's positioned over the road cut the right way. Fuck him, I think. Stupid old prick.

I do the job. Hamm raises the back bucket. I open the hatch and hot asphalt pours out. I jam it closed. De Carlo comes over with a hard rake. Hamm sits in the truck. De Carlo pulls and pushes the asphalt. I grab a hard rake, too. My work is never good enough for De Carlo. He goes over what I do. Fuck him; I don't care. The old fool starts the BOMAG. I grab the bucket and slop oil on the roller with the brush to keep the asphalt from sticking. The heat coming off the asphalt singes the side of my face.

Hamm comes back. "Nice work. Nice work, De Carlo."

What the fuck, I think. What about me and my oil brush? I think about jamming it up Hamm's ass.

Twenty minutes later, we're done. De Carlo runs the BOMAG back onto the trailer. Hamm backs the truck up. De Carlo hitches the trailer to the truck; another job I can't be trusted to do. I wipe sweat from my face with my orange fluorescent T-shirt. It smears black. We all walk around and get in the cab of the truck.

"You ever read Dostoevsky?" I ask Hamm.

"What? What the fuck?"

"Forget about it."

"Watch your hole, son."

De Carlo looks out the window. Then he speaks: "Coffee."

I take mine to go and sit against the back of the building in the shade. I've got fifteen minutes away from Hamm and De Carlo. I watch seagulls and crows by the dumpster. The seagulls are aggressive, the crows more strategic. Both species will inherit the earth once we're gone. They'll fight for dominance. I'd put my money on the crows. One day a crow Dostoevsky will write masterfully about the misery of the crow world, about the stupidity of seagulls, about the myth of humans. This idea makes me smile. I drink my coffee, eat a doughnut and watch the crows. I want to join them, become a black bastard crow waiting for all humanity to burn and die.

ASPHALT

Back in the truck, Hamm has news for us.

"I'll drop you both at the next job. I'll drop half a tonne of asphalt. You can take care of it. It's a small job, out of the way. I'm doing it for you. The bosses won't find you. Take your time. Take the rest of the morning. I'll be back in plenty of time to pick you up for dinner."

By dinner he means lunch. It's city-worker talk. The rest of it is code for he wants to go bang his girlfriend. Hamm is married. He's also about fifty-five years old. I know his son Warren but he doesn't know this. I used to play hockey with Warren. I wonder whether Warren knows his old man fucks around. Then I wonder who his girlfriend is, who would fuck this old, smelly man in an asphalt truck. She must be out there. There must be others like her. Maybe one will fuck me. Who knows.

De Carlo doesn't say anything to Hamm. What can he say? I stay silent, too.

Hamm drops us off on a quiet residential street with the BOMAG, the hard rakes, my oil bucket and brush, and half a tonne of asphalt. We do the job while Hamm goes and fucks his girlfriend.

After, De Carlo goes and takes a nap under a tree. He doesn't care who sees him. I walk away, stroll down the street and look around. There's not much to see. The street is still. Kids at school. Parents working or staying inside, out of the heat. Safe, comfortable-looking houses. There's nothing here. At least not on the surface. Behind the beautiful lawns, pristine paint jobs, and smooth, black-topped driveways is something evil. I can feel it. I walk around and feel it for half an hour. I'm like a crow surveying this drab neighbourhood. But there is nothing shiny here so I go back to the job site.

De Carlo is awake, sitting at the curb.

"He should be back," he says.

I can't believe De Carlo spoke to me. What a fucking shocker.

I don't say anything and hang around the finished job, waiting for Hamm to get back.

Hamm's got a big idiot grin on his face when he returns. But he's also all in a rush.

"We'll be late for dinner. Let's shake a leg."

De Carlo doesn't move any faster than usual. Shake a leg means nothing to him. I move a bit faster, but whatever I do is not good enough for Hamm.

"Come on, son; get your ass in gear."

"Caw! Caw!" I fire back.

Hamm looks confused for a second. Then he goes, "Watch it, son. I could get you reassigned. You like weeds? I'll get Reece over here and dump you with the weed whackers."

I put the hard rakes on the truck, hang the bucket and brush off a hook, and get in the cab.

After dinner it feels like a sauna when I step out of the air-conditioned lunchroom into the afternoon heat. Fifteen minutes later we're at our afternoon job, but no one wants to get out of the truck. I look at De Carlo. He's fallen asleep. Hamm just sits there, staring out the windshield. I've got nothing to say.

Hamm comes up with this: "Let's finish this job and then go for a beer."

De Carlo wakes up.

ASPHALT

Hamm asks him, "Your friend still live around the corner? Remember we dropped that half tonne so he could top his driveway? That's still worth a beer on a hot day like this. Let's get this done, boys, and then go have a cold beer."

De Carlo doesn't speak. He shuffles out of the cab and I follow. My feet burn in my boots. The asphalt stinks and the fumes nearly overwhelm me. My hardhat feels like a magnifying glass, concentrating the sun's rays on my scalp. Sweat drips off me as we do the job. We get it done. It's about two o'clock and thirty-five degrees, much hotter on an asphalt crew. I've had enough.

Hamm says, "Time for a fucking ale."

De Carlo wipes his sweaty face. "Yes," he says.

We drive around the corner. De Carlo goes and gets his friend. We walk around back of his house. Grape vines hang above our heads from a pergola. The interlock at our feet is immaculate. Gino, De Carlo's buddy, comes out with a six-pack of 50. He wears sandals on top of work socks, green work pants, a baggy, faded black T-shirt on his squat upper body, and an old straw hat. He looks like one of the guys from the cement crew. Maybe he's retired city. I don't know. All I know is I want that beer. Eventually, after the two senior men are served, I get one. It's piss-warm but I don't care.

"Thanks."

Gino ignores me. He tips his 50 back and speaks in Italian with De Carlo.

Hamm looks around the yard.

I drink my beer fast. So does Hamm. We're both done long before De Carlo and Gino. They sit on lawn chairs, nursing their beers, gesturing as they jabber.

Hamm looks impatient for another beer. Gino notices but doesn't do anything about it. Only when De Carlo is finished his beer does Gino get up and offer the last two beers from the six-pack to De Carlo and Hamm, in that order. I stand there. Where's my second beer? I look at Gino. He shrugs his shoulders, mutters something in Italian and goes back to his lawn chair, folding his empty hands in his lap.

This is bullshit. I want to walk away, leave Hamm and De Carlo, but I can't do that. How would I get back to the yard? Hamm and De Carlo—what a couple of pricks. They really are.

I do the only thing I can do. I walk back out to the street and get into the truck. The *Toronto Sun* is still there. I flip to Anastasia. Maybe it's the heat but I swear she's got a copy of *Crime and Punishment* open, that she's reading it with a contented smile on her face, her breasts still nice and round, still real.

A crow calls from a tree.

I call back—"Caw! Caw!"

Hamm and De Carlo appear.

"What the fuck is that noise?" Hamm asks.

"Caw! Caw!" I say, right in his face.

De Carlo snorts.

"That's it. You're finished here. Hope you'll like weeds, son," Hamm says, putting the truck in gear.

"Caw! Caw!"

I wish I could fly right out De Carlo's open window.

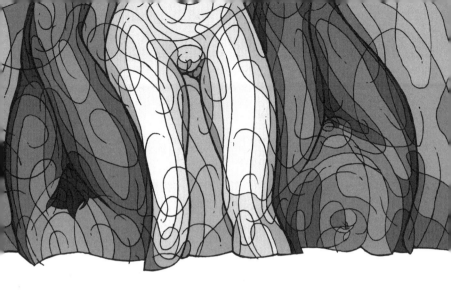

THREE WOMEN ON THE BUS

Sean sits in his favourite row of seats on a very crowded bus. He can't concentrate on his crossword, but not because of the driver's aggressive accelerating and braking. That rarely bothers him. It is the three women no more than a metre away. They are talking about hair removal. One of them had a haircut recently. That started the conversation:

Girl one (*a black girl seated on the bus*): "I love your hair. You get it done?"

Girl two (*a white girl standing in the aisle, leaning over her friend*): "Yeah, a couple days ago."

G1: "Where?"

G2: "Philippe's, on King Edward."

Girl three (*also black; she also stands in the aisle*): "Where's that at? I don't know it."

G2: "Close to Laurier. It's a little place. I think it's only been open less than a year. This is my third time."

G1: "It's beautiful."

G2: "Thanks, girl."

G1: "Get your eyebrows done, too?"

G2: "Oh yeah. You know I have to stay on top of that or I end up looking like a mountain man."

G1 (*laughing and smoothing out her eyebrows with a finger*): "Yeah. I know what you mean. Me too, girl."

G2: "And I took it even further this time."

G3: "What? What're you talking about?"

G2 (*nodding toward her waist*): "Down there. I got it all done. Just a couple days ago."

G3 (*looking down and then up quickly*): "You did?" (*And then more quietly*) "Fuck, girl, all of it?"

G2 (*smiling*): "All of it. The whole way, girl. Fuckin' Brazilian! What else you gonna do? You gonna do something like that, you go all the way."

G1 (*coolly*): "I've been getting it done for a long time now. All of it. But I do it myself at home. I never had someone do it for me." She looks over at the other black girl.

G3: "Why?"

G2: "It makes me feel cleaner, ya know? Nothing gets in the way."

G3: "I never done it. Bikini lines is all…it don't itch?"

G1: "No, sister, they take it right down. It's not like shaving. We're talking all the way."

Girl three looks around the bus.

G2: "Yeah, it's sick. And my boyfriend fuckin' loves it."

G3: "You don't think that's a little fucked up?"

G2: "Come on, girl; get with it. Everyone does it now. Makes it easier for the loving, you know. Nothing gets caught. No cleaning jizz out of your patch, you know? It's not just about him. I love it too, girl. Everything is just that much *smoother*." She laughs.

Girl three looks unsure. She looks around the bus. Her eyes hit Sean. He holds her stare for a second and then she looks away.

The girls don't say anything else while the bus pulls into Hurdman Station. Half the passengers get off, transferring to other routes. The three girls move to the back of the bus. Sean turns and watches them go. He riffles the crossword with his thumb, staring at their asses as they walk. Sean knows two of them remove all of their pubic hair and that the other one does not.

Sean watches the girls sit down in the open seats near the back of the bus and start talking. They are now out of his hearing range. Who knows what they're talking about? Sean doesn't. But maybe he knows enough about them. He looks at the girls closely. They are half his age, maybe younger. They are not women compared to him; they are truly girls.

Sean thinks about his ex-wife. They have been divorced six years. He can barely recall what her "patch" looked like; he really can't. Sean knows his ex-wife never shaved it or waxed it. He remembers that much.

He has not had sex in three years. He had a short-lived relationship with a woman from work. It was not very satisfying. He has not seen, touched, felt, or penetrated a naked woman since. This is no way for a forty-four-year-old man to live. This is not living of any kind—listening to young women talk about their pubic hair on the bus.

Now there are no pretty women nearby on the bus. He should forget about the three girls at the back, forget about what they do with their pubic hair.

Sean turns and looks at other passengers. He needs something to take him in a different direction. Blank faces. Heads tilted back, rocking slightly to iPod music. Some with noses in newspapers. Others gaze out dirty bus windows.

His stop is coming up. He is supposed to go to work. The three women are still at the back of the bus. He looks down at the crossword puzzle. Sean sees that he has scrawled all over it, blurred out all the words in a black, inky mess. The bus rolls on.

GREEKS

I see them in the corridor and on the stairwell outside my flat. They grin at me. They snicker and laugh and mutter in their language. I don't recognize it, but my wife says it's Greek. She is probably right. Back in Hamilton, her parents have Greek neighbours. These guys look Greek. My neighbours in Hamilton are Italian. I know Italian when I hear it, but not Greek. A lot of Greeks and Italians look a bit the same: that swarthy, manicured, Southern European sheen. But what do I know?

They live in the flat above us. They moved in a couple months ago. At first it was quiet, but then the noise started. The building is old, the floors bow and creak. I hear them walk above me. I hear the music they play: awful Eurotrash disco, the worst of the European song competition dross.

I was up there last night. I knocked on their door. It took a long time for them to answer. When they did, they were both at the door, grinning and snickering at me.

"I live downstairs. Underneath you."

31

"Yes."

"The music. Your music. It's too loud."

"Iss no too loud."

"It's too loud. Believe me. I live downstairs. I can hear it plain as day."

"Iss no too loud."

One of them snickered and said something to the other one in Greek.

"It's too fucking loud and it's bothering me. Turn it down."

"Iss no too loud."

"Look, stop fucking saying that and go in there and turn the music down. Turn it down or I'm calling the estate agent."

They looked worried.

"We turn it down."

"It's crap music anyway."

I looked at them grinning at me.

"You guys are a cliché, listening to that shitty Eurotrash disco."

They looked confused.

"Whaz this mean, cliché? It don't sound nice."

"Look it up."

That stopped their grinning. They closed their door. I stood there, waiting. The music went off. I went back downstairs to my flat. I sat in my living room, reading a book. I sipped a beer, paused, and listened. There was no music any more, not a sound coming from upstairs. It was dead quiet in the building. My wife was out at the pub. She had called earlier to say something about going out for a drink after work.

GREEKS

...

I see them all over town—in Tesco, at the chemist, the post office, the Cellar Bar on Tuesday nights. Sometimes they see me, other times they don't. They are always together. They might be brothers; I don't know. When they see me, they grin but never speak. That is, unless I talk to them first.

I am downstairs in the building's foyer collecting my mail from the pile the postie pushed through the slot. The mail comes early here, between seven and seven-thirty. It's one of the highlights of my day: rummaging through the mail, looking for news on my writing, a letter from home, anything. There is one lousy letter today, and my BT bill. The Greeks appear. I am startled. I am in my pyjamas and slippers. They are fully dressed, on their way out very early. Where are they going? I make eye contact and they stop. They don't snicker this morning. They look sober and serious. It forces me to pause.

I ask, "You looking for your mail?"

The Greeks stare at me. Do they think I mess with their mail? I'm not sure what's going on.

"I know that word now."

"Eh?"

I want to go upstairs. I feel vulnerable in my pyjamas, exposed.

"You call us cliché. I talk to people. I look it up. Iss no nice what you say."

They're right about that.

"You should apologize to us."

They stand there, expectantly. I shuffle the two envelopes in

33

my hand. I scratch my left knee through the thin material of my pyjamas. The Greeks want an apology, but I don't give them one.

"Where you from?" one of them asks. "You not sound Scottish."

"Canada."

Now the grins return. One of them exclaims, "Oh! Can-AH-DAH. Now we know. Now we know."

"What the fuck is that supposed to mean?"

They laugh and talk in Greek.

I start getting pissed with them again. "Hey, I said what the fuck is wrong with that?"

They stop laughing. They look serious again. One of them says, "You say fuck all-ah time. Is that cliché? Are you cliché?"

They start laughing their asses off now. "Are you a Can-AH-DAH cliché?"

I feel disarmed. I need to get away. I blurt, "Just keep the fucking noise down and there won't be any problems, got it?"

They both look at me and grin. I turn away, head up the stairs back to my flat. I close the door, throw the envelopes down on a table, and go for coffee. My wife is gone. She went for a run or something. The flat is deadly quiet once more.

• • •

At four o'clock in the morning I wake up to thumping and banging. I sit up in bed. I'm alone and confused. It's pitch black in my flat. My wife is not here. She's in Sheffield or some place for a work conference. More thumping and banging. The walls shake and vibrate from the impact. What the fuck? What the fuck are those Greeks up to now?

I sit up in the centre of my bed. BANG! It sounds like someone is being thrown against the wall. I jump out of bed. There is a loud thud against the floor right above me. I search for my slippers. I've had it with the Greeks. This is ridiculous. I'm wide awake. I grab my keys so I won't lock myself out and storm out the door, up the stairs. I bang on their door with my right fist. I hear more thumping and banging. I hammer on the door when there is a break in the noise. It goes quiet. I pound on the door some more. I knock five or six times. It is quiet and calm, but I am enraged. The Greeks don't come to the door. I press my nose in the door jam and holler: "I know you're in there! Open the fucking door!"

Silence.

I bang some more. "Open it, you fuckers. You Greek fuckers!"

It's futile. They are not coming to the door. I kick their door and then go back to my flat. I can't sleep. I make coffee and sit in the bay window, looking out on the street. There is no more noise from upstairs, not even the sound of feet walking across the ceiling. The Greeks have shut it down completely.

. . .

I see them late the next day when I come back from the post office. I stop them on the concrete stairs of our building. I'm enraged again.

"What was all that noise in the middle of the night?"

I didn't get enough sleep. I'm overtired and grumpy.

"What the fuck were you guys doing?"

They look at me meekly.

"You didn't answer your door. You must have fucking heard me banging on it."

One of the Greeks says, "We were worried. We didn't want to open the door. You sounded very angry."

"I *was* fucking angry. You woke me up and I never got back to sleep. It sounded like you were throwing each other around up there. What the fuck was that all about?"

The grins come back.

"You say *fuck* too much. You should try and stop. Iss cliché."

I look at the swarthy Greek fucker who said it. "Fuck that," I say.

It makes him laugh and he relaxes a little.

"We were wrestling. That is all."

"Wrestling? What the fuck. At four in the morning? What kind of a fucked up thing is that to do?"

"Yess. We just wrestle."

"Another fucking cliché," I fire back. "Keep it the fuck down or I'm calling the estate agent." I push past them into the building.

• • •

Early the next morning, I sit at the table by the bay window drinking tepid coffee. There are no buildings here over four storeys. I look out on the town. I'm like a nosey old woman scouring the street. It's quiet in the flat, in the entire building. My wife has gone to Dundee for the day. I didn't see her before she left. She took the bus early this morning with a woman from France who she works with. They're going shopping. I go sometimes but not today. I like the Virgin Megastore but nothing else about Dundee. It reminds me too much of Hamilton and Windsor. It's the teenaged pregnancy capital of the UK, possibly all of Europe. The pimply-faced moms and dads pushing prams depress me. If you're still using Clearasil at night, you're too young to be a parent. The moms all look bitchy and tough. The dads tougher still, dressed in dark blue, Umbro shell-suits, trainers untied, sideways caps, sucking on fags, chewing on toothpicks or guzzling tins of lager. They skulk and trawl the high street, faces greasy from the chemical ooze of the drugs they gobble. And the entire city stinks—from the oil refineries, puke, piss, and dog shit. I can live without Dundee today.

Here they come. The Greeks. Back from an early trip to Tesco. I assumed they were sleeping still, that that was why it is quiet upstairs. But no, they are up early. Their hands are loaded with carrier bags. They grin and yammer to each other as they walk down the pavement toward our building. It is a sunny and bright morning. The Greeks each wear black toques and black ski jackets, even though it is not really that cold. Another cliché: overdressed continental Europeans who think the East Coast of Scotland is the coldest place on earth. It's likely plus four or five degrees, which is not cold, not by Canadian standards. I want to tell the Greeks that they don't know cold; that they should come to Canada and they will experience real cold. But now I'm thinking in clichés. I huff at the sight of the Greeks. I should have gone to Dundee with my wife. I feel like I haven't seen her in weeks. For a moment, as the sun reflects up off a puddle on the street into my face, my mind fogs and I can't picture what my wife's face looks like. What does she look like? Where is she?

"Fucking Greeks," I mutter, as I sip my now lukewarm coffee.

...

The thumping and banging starts again. I jerk up in bed and immediately feel dizzy. My wife is not in bed. Where is she? She must be watching TV or in the washroom. BANG! It sounds like someone dropped an anvil on the floor above me. Then the lower thumping noises start again. Then BANG! Another anvil. Or the impact of demolition. Is that what's going on? Are those fucking Greeks demolishing the flat above me? Wrestling? That's not wrestling. There's more going on up there.

I put on shoes and stomp up the stairs to their flat. This time my pounding is answered right away. Their door flies open. The two Greeks stand in front of me, almost naked, sweaty, their bodies strangely hairless. They wear only loincloths. No joke: loincloths. The fucking Greeks wear loincloths. I step back and shake my head. They sneer at me and then grin.

"What the fuck?"

The Greeks stand there, breathing hard, sweating.

"What the fuck is going on? I mean, really—what the fuck is going on? What are you wearing?"

"Iss no your business what we do, what we wear."

"Yeah but...CHRIST!"

One of the Greeks steps toward me. They are uncharacteristically aggressive.

"What you want?"

"The noise! The fucking banging! What the fuck are you doing in there? More wrestling?" I lean, strain to look past them into their flat.

"Iss no your business."

"Fucking right it is. It's my fucking business when I'm right below you trying to sleep."

Now both Greeks are really close to me. I can smell the garlic in their sweat.

"You faggot?" one Greek asks quickly.

I'm stunned. "What? What the fuck?"

"You faggot? Iss simple question. Iss that why you bang on our door?" The Greek who asked snickers to the other one. He says, "*Pousti.*" They both laugh.

I want to grab the fucker, yank him out into the corridor and beat the shit out of him. I've wanted to do it for a long time. But where do I grab him? They're both wearing loincloths and are slick with sweat.

I stab a finger at the Greeks one at a time, at both their bald chests. "I'm not a faggot, get it. And so what if I was? You fucking Greeks should know there's nothing wrong with that. And besides, you're the fuckers who are pretty much naked, sweaty, making a fuck-load of noise like you've been fucking each other up the ass for the past hour. You're the ones who look like faggots, not me!"

"We no faggots. We brothers. We just wrestle."

My head spins.

"What? What the fuck? What's with this wrestling shit? I don't believe it. At four in the morning? You wrestle in the middle of the night?"

The Greeks shrug their sweaty shoulders.

"How old are you two?"

"I twenty-two. He twenty-three. We brothers. We wrestle. You no wrestle with your brother?"

I look at the Greek who answered. "You've got to be kidding. Yeah, I wrestled with my brother. When I was a fucking kid! Not now. Not as an adult. There's a big difference."

Again the Greeks shrug their shoulders.

"And you're keeping me and my wife awake!"

Now the Greeks raise their eyebrows rather than shrug their shoulders.

Now what the fuck, I wonder.

"Your wife? Where your wife? We no see your wife. Where is she?" They grin and snicker.

"She's downstairs," I answer feebly.

"Yess? We no see her. We see only you. We only ever see you. You follow us around—to the Tesco. To the post office. To the Cellar bar. You look at us. You sit in window and watch us. You come upstairs in the night to see us. You must be faggot. And we no see your wife."

I've had it. I reel back and throw a haymaker at the Greek who called me a faggot. I miss his head. My punch hits his sweaty shoulder and deflects off into the plaster. My fist gets stuck for a second. The Greeks are quick. The other Greek grabs me by the arm and wrenches it behind my head, half-Nelson style. It hurts like fuck. I go to elbow him in the ribs with my one free arm but the other Greek stops me. They both hold me. They bring me down. I grunt and resist, kicking and scratching, but the Greeks are too much for me. They are wrestlers, after all. The one Greek sits on my chest, his knees pinning my arms back like we used to do on the playground. His stinking, loinclothed Greek crotch is right in my face.

"Get the fuck off me!" I bang my heels on the floor. "FUCK!"

"You say fuck too much," the Greeks say in unison. They laugh at me.

I shake my head back and forth, close my eyes and bear down, trying to summon the strength to shake the two nearly naked Greeks off.

Then I feel them relax their hold on me. I open my eyes and there's my wife wearing only an old T-shirt. Lying on the floor, I can see up her T-shirt easily. She is wearing white panties. Where did she come from?

"What the fuck?" she says.

The Greeks get off me and snicker. One of them says, "Yess. Ah yess. Your wife. She from Can-AH-DAH too? She say fuck all ah time, too? We hear her say it before."

The Greeks stand in their doorway.

"Fuck you, Greeks," I manage.

"Go back downstairs," my wife says. "You're making an ass of yourself. You've lost it this time."

"I'm calling the estate agent on those two," I point up at the Greeks from where I lie on the floor.

"Who cares?" one Greek says. "Fuck the estate agent. Iss our flat. We pay rent. We just wrestle."

My wife looks pissed. But she helps me up off the floor. I stand there, wiping crumbs and crap off my pyjamas. The Greeks stand defiant in their loincloths.

"Fucking Greeks," I say low, as my wife leads me down the stairs to our flat.

I look at her closely.

"Where have you been? I feel like I haven't seen you in weeks."

She peers at me. "What? What the fuck are you talking about? Are you accusing me of something? Seriously—what the fuck are you saying? You've been obsessing over things too much."

"Like the Greeks?"

"Yeah, like the Greeks. They have names, you know: Peter and Paul. They're brothers. Did you know that? They're decent people. They like to have fun. I know them."

I look at my wife. Fun? What is she talking about, fun? Did I hear her correctly? Am I imagining things? I haven't had fun in weeks. Maybe months or years or my entire fucking life.

I look closely at my wife but she seems blurry again, her face, her features, her body—all of it seems unfamiliar. I go to speak but stop. I don't know whom I'm talking to. Is she here? Where has she been? With the Greeks? I'm not even sure my wife is here with me now. I grab the banister that leads downstairs to our flat and hold it as tightly as I can with both hands.

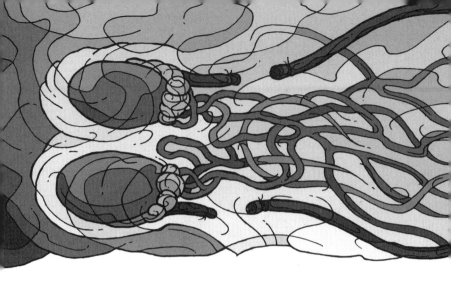

PROCEDURE

The procedure calls for me to take a Valium an hour beforehand. I'm disappointed when the pharmacist dispenses exactly one Valium. I thought I'd get at least three or four, to dull the pain afterward, or as compensation for what I'm undergoing.

I just finished reading a novel about a heroin addict. Valium, or, more correctly, diazepam, is cited in the book as a recreational drug the narrator used when he could not score smack. For me, a few Valium over the coming days would be great. I don't deal well with pain and tend to exaggerate suffering. But I get one and only one, a very small pill that looks like nothing to get excited about.

In a small grocery store, I buy a 500 mL bottle of orange juice. I slug back the dull blue pill right in the store. I go back out into the cold and walk across the street to kill some time in a used bookstore, before going to the doctor's office. I start to feel stoned fifteen minutes later and use the handrail when I climb the stairs to the second floor of the bookstore. I buy a paperback J.M. Coetzee novel and pay for it with change, slowly counting out seven dollars and thirty-five cents. The bookstore clerk says something to me about the novel but I can't make sense of his words.

I walk up Bank Street and look for my wife, who is driving to meet me. The bus drivers are on strike, Christmas is a week away, and the streets brim with snow—everything is moving slowly. On diazepam, it's funny how the cars seem to plod along. I stand on a street corner like an idiot and watch cars, hoping to see my wife.

It takes a while to realize the ringing noise is the phone in my pocket. I don't carry a cell phone. My wife gave me hers, thinking, because of the procedure, that I should have it. I'm not sure how it's supposed to help. The Valium is more useful. A guy walks past and leers at me, standing on the corner in the cold, glazed over as I gauge the oncoming cars, while I ignore the ringing in my pocket. I snap out of it and answer the phone. My wife is just leaving her office, but she is not going to make it to see me before the procedure. She wishes me well. I mumble something and then shamble across the street to the doctor's.

I have to shit. Valium or not, I'm nervous. In the doctor's office, I check in, take off my winter boots and coat.

"Is there a washroom I can use?" I ask the young woman working the front desk. She seems too casually dressed to be working in a doctor's office. She wears a tight green sweater and low-cut, faded jeans.

"Yeah, but can you hold on a sec?"

I can't but I will. What choice do I have? If I shit my pants, I will have to leave.

The woman goes away to see about something and then reappears.

"Down the hall, take a right, last door on your left."

Sedated, it's too much information for me. I go where she pointed and figure it out. I take a horribly wretched shit—from the drug, the nerves; I don't know why. It's something out of the ordinary for me. I don't usually shit in public, in the afternoon, on unfamiliar toilets.

Back in the waiting room I flip through magazines, unable to focus or read. A post-procedural patient comes out, walking like a man might with a knife shoved up his ass. His wife stands. The casually dressed girl comes over with a kit and explains what the man should do to recover and what he should not do.

"No sex for a week," she says flatly.

The man's wife puts her hand on his knee. He looks down at the hand but does not react. He looks completely stoned, unable to comprehend anything. The girl speaks mostly to the wife. Then she gives the man a can of ginger ale and tells him to wait fifteen minutes before leaving.

Someone else comes into the office but it's not my wife. It's another man and his wife or girlfriend. They speak French and I understand little of what is said; fucked up on diazepam or not, my French is not good. My wife is still not here.

A minute later the doctor calls to the girl to bring me in.

"Mr. Firth, this way," she says.

A magazine slides from my hands to the floor. I follow the girl, watching her ass in her low-cut jeans. I am about to have a vasectomy so it seems right to summon a primal yet misdirected sexual urge before having my nuts sliced open. She is gone before I know it and then it is just Dr. Walsh.

"Did you wear your support?" he asks.

"Yes."

"Good. Take down your pants and everything else to your ankles and lie on the table."

Again, it's too much information. He repeats the instructions. I fumble around. I expect stirrups and having to remove everything. Instead, he wants my legs together.

"Did you forget to shave?"

"It's the best I could do."

I had tried the night before—after having sex with my wife for the last time for a week—to shave my scrotum but it is such an unnatural thing to do. My pubic area—that I could handle. But even with the surgical razor they supplied that does not come anywhere close to the skin, shaving my balls was tough. My wife offered to help. If she had offered before we fucked, as some kind of kinky foreplay, I might have accepted. But after coming and then cleaning up, I decided I was the only one fit to put a razor anywhere near my scrotum. My whole life I have protected my nuts. To put a sharp instrument millimetres from the soft flesh that holds my testicles was an anathema, as far as I was concerned. I did what I could but my best is not good enough for Dr. Walsh.

He quickly and aggressively shaves my nuts. I feel like a sheep being sheared. I begin to feel the diazepam wear off, or at least not stand up to what was coming. Next he grabs my cock and wraps an elastic band around it. I stare at the boring landscape painting on the ceiling and try to think of anything else.

"This will be the worst of it," he says. "A sharp blast of freezing that feels like a pinch."

I recoil, groaning. It's more like having my nuts in a vice.

"The next two will not be as bad."

He's right about this.

"Another sharp one."

No shit. I hold my breath. The happy Valium high is long gone.

"Relax. I'll just give that a minute to take."

He's over at a desk fucking around with something. And then he's back on me. It feels like he's pouncing, like he takes some pleasure in this. He must; how else could he do this all day?

"Just hold still. This is a sterile cloth."

He lays it on me.

"Keep your hands on your chest. This will take a few minutes. You'll feel some pulling, some tugging."

I don't like the sound of it but what choice do I have? I clench my fingers together on my chest, close my eyes and try to ride it out.

My wife is in the waiting room when it's over. She does her best to be sympathetic. It does not come easily to her. I am handed a can of ginger ale. I get the same spiel from the girl about no sex for a week, no heavy lifting, and to send a sample in the mail in three months. Jerking off into a vial so someone can test my spunk for signs of life is the furthest thing from my mind. I sip ginger ale through a bendy straw and slouch in a chair.

My wife wants to go. My appointment started early, so we are ahead of schedule. I am supposed to wait fifteen minutes before leaving and it has been maybe ten minutes since I sat down with my ginger ale. My wife is restless. She is worried about the bad traffic, the bus strike, and the snow.

We head out. She drives. I feel lethargic and vaguely sore, like I just had the shit kicked out of me and was dumped at the curb for the garbagemen to sort out.

We have a jumbled conversation in the car. She apologizes for being late. I watch pedestrians struggle over snowbanks the ploughs have left behind. We stop and buy something for dinner. I go home, take off my boots and coat, mutter a few words to my children and their sitter, and then head upstairs to bed with a book. I don't read a word. I sleep for two hours and then wake confused, feeling hungover and hazy. I eat pizza and lie on the sofa, watching television until two A.M.

• • •

The next morning, my wife is gone by the time I get up. My kids are downstairs watching television, eating dry cereal. I stagger down and make coffee. I take an anti-inflammatory and wish again for Valium.

I pull on pants on top of pyjama bottoms, winter boots over bare feet, slip on my coat, and struggle to get the kids to school. I walk back home, fall onto the sofa and put on the television.

The phone rings. I expect my wife, calling to check on me. But it isn't my wife. It's my director from work, his voice strained. He knows I'm taking a day or two off to recover from the procedure. His call is unexpected. I'm not sure how to react. He tells me—fairly soon after some preliminary talk about how I'm feeling—that he has bad news. My mind races. Then he tells me a work colleague in the office next to mine—a man younger than me—died the night before from an apparent heart attack. I'm stunned. The dead man is also a friend. I talk a bit longer to my director, repeating my astonishment several times. It is unbelievable, it really is.

I thank my director for his call. I put down the telephone and shuffle around my house in a daze, trying to make sense of the news. I get nowhere with it.

My balls hurt and my head aches. I think about the telephone call, about the horrible news. I think about my co-worker, now dead. I had lunch with him forty-eight hours ago at some insipid meeting, a huge waste of time. It was the last time I saw him, at that stupid—terribly stupid—meeting. I guess he went to work the day after, the day I had my vasectomy. Another day at the office. That is no way for a life to end.

I stop thinking about the procedure. I'm not worried about killing the pain in my nuts any more—it's the thought of a dead man I want to chase from my head. I go into my kitchen, rummage around in a bowl of containers of pills. I find codeine I was prescribed for a tooth extraction a year or so ago. I put three in my mouth and wash them down with a double shot of neat whisky. Then I step cautiously into the rest of my day.

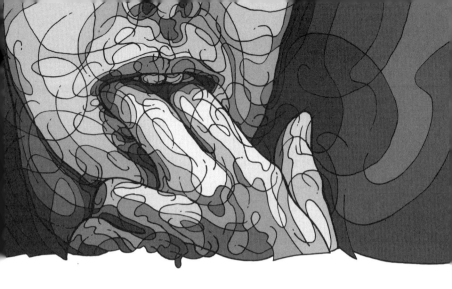

THE LUNCH PROGRAM

The idea is to eat as fast as you can, then go out to the old HAAA grounds and fuck around before school starts again. That's exactly what we do.

Cliff's got cigarettes. His older sister Stephanie buys them. She's in grade eight. Me, Cliff, Johnny, and Glenn are all in grade seven. Stephanie's got some friends who hang around but it's her I like. She's hot. Filipino, beautiful black hair, lips pucker when she inhales.

Stephanie gives Cliff smokes. He passes them out. My hands sweat as he goes around the circle with his lighter. I worry I won't get mine lighted, that I'll look like a loser. The thing is, at this age, you can never let on you don't know what's going on. Cigarettes, alcohol, sex, female bodily functions, minor thievery, delinquent acts of violence and vandalism—you have to be savvy to all of it. No, more than savvy; you have to make the impression that you're with it, that you've done it, that you'd do it—whatever *it* is—right away. You're always ready, always on the edge, being tested. It's exhausting. But you have to look relaxed at the same time. On the walk home, when I split with Glenn at the corner of Herkimer Street and Dundurn, I slouch home and try to be a kid again—alone, fucking around in me and my brother's bedroom with goddamned Tonka trucks or some shit. That's how wiped I am.

But if I can pull this off, there's a chance I'll get to kiss Stephanie's dark lips and grab her ass—that beautiful ass, stuffed into her tight Roadrunner jeans. Because she watches us, measuring us against the others. Cliff knows we like his sister. Sometimes he acts protective, other times he acts more like her pimp, like he gets off on all the attention paid to her and, by default, to him.

"Matt. Come closer. The fuckin' wind."

We huddle under a basketball net.

"Come 'ere. You gotta get closer."

I step up. Peripherally, I see Stephanie check me out. I jut my chin forward, offering the cigarette to Cliff. He cups his hands over it like a pro and I do my best to inhale at the right time with the right force to get it lighted, while trying to keep my cool. I pull it off and then step back. I blow smoke over my left shoulder and casually eye Stephanie. She's not looking anymore. Now she's yakking with one of her friends. What the fuck.

So I stand around with Cliff, Johnny, and Glenn, looking the part. I smoke it down to the filter then stamp out the butt. By then, the girls have fucked off over to a park bench near Tuckett Street.

We head over. Hands stuffed in pockets. Shoulders wrenched forward. Not saying much. Nodding gestures. Stupid, idiot grins.

Cliff's our in. He goes, "Steph, what-chu hangin' out here for? Why'd you fuck off?"

The rest of us bob our heads like broken puppets, agreeing with his questions.

The girls giggle and wait for Stephanie to answer.

She pauses and then goes, "Take your boys somewheres else, Cliffy. We got shit to do. We got shit to talk about. Grade eight shit. Don't concern yous. Go on—shoo."

She waves her hand at us. I watch her fingers like they're moving in slow motion. Her brown digits fan toward me, then brush me away. I feel the air they push. I smell it. It's scented with cigarettes, sweet perfume, and the salami she had on her sandwich at lunch. I see myself catch her fingers in my mouth, licking them, sucking them, biting them—searing them off and taking them home in my mouth to my corner of the bedroom. I'd roll onto my bed, pull back my pillow, open my mouth and let her fingers fall out. I'd watch them: four fingers from her right hand lying on my bed sheet. No blood; I sucked it away. Just her beautiful, languorous fingers. I'd be up all night staring at them. Smelling them. Tasting them. Feeling them. Taking them up, running them over my body. But in the morning, I'd pop them back in my mouth, take them to school and give them back to Stephanie. She'd be waiting for me at the doors to the school, her fingerless right hand held up stump-like. I'd walk over, open my mouth and her fingers would walk out, across my tongue, and then settle back on her hand. The taste of her; I'd hold that inside me all day.

Cliff goes, "Yeah, you're all such hot shit. Don't got time for us, eh?"

I don't even see the other girls, only Stephanie. She shoos us again. I watch her fingers. It's a film now, running and re-running in my head: her fingers coming at me, me grabbing them, biting them off and slinking away with them in my mouth, like a dog with a bone. I can barely hold myself back from chomping a chunk out of her. She looks like chocolate. She smells like fresh meat. She moves like maple syrup. The fingers first, then her hands, arms, eyes, tits, legs, feet—I'd save her ass for last. Eat her up, put her inside me fully, completely. But I'd let her out at night—open my mouth, let her fall onto my pillow. I'd have all her parts. I'd scattered them, her a puzzle of parts on my bed. Sometimes I'd put her back together. Other times I'd leave her in pieces. Maybe just enjoy her ass, just her feet, just her lips—smoke her fingers like cigarettes.

Cliff cuffs my shoulder and brings me out of it. "Matt. What the fuck. Quit yer fuckin' staring. That's my sister, you idiot. Your mom never tell you it's rude to stare?"

I look at Cliff. Then at Stephanie. She laughs into her hand and turns away from me. I shrug and walk back to the basketball court for another smoke before school starts.

• • •

After school I tell Glenn I gotta get my hair cut at Joe's over on Locke Street. It's a lie but he buys it.

I walk toward Locke but then turn right onto Pearl Street instead, go down the hill to Bold Street, then back up the rise on the other side to the old wooden bridge over the train tracks. I look around and see no one watching. I climb up and over the eight-foot chain-link fence, then hunker down on the other side where the bridge cuts into a slope of earth. I settle in the wet, rotten leaves, busted bottles, muddy grocery bags, and general filth like a troll, waiting for Stephanie.

• • •

The last month in the lunch program I've paid close attention to Stephanie eating. I can't take my eyes away. Every bite she takes holds me. We sit around in desks, our brown-bag lunches laid out in front of us. We're not supposed to talk. Just eat up and then we're cut loose.

Mr. Boudreau supervises the program. He sits at the front in his desk, rifling through papers, doing his best to ignore us while letting us know that bullshit will not be tolerated. He's a prick of a teacher anyway, like most.

I chew my Cheez-Whiz-on-white-bread sandwich and look at Stephanie. Her sandwiches are way more interesting than mine. Dark bread. Real meat. Chunks of real cheese gushing out the sides. My sandwiches are boring, bland, white bread, white-boy things. Bologna is about as exotic as it gets for me. Egg salad. Peanut butter and jelly. The usual shit. Stephanie brings fruit I can't identify. Crazy-looking plums or something. I get Macintosh apples, and maybe homemade cookies in waxed paper.

I watch Stephanie bite and chew, bite and chew. Her dark fingers wrap around rye and salami. Her bright white teeth flash. I focus on her lips, moving somewhat circularly, devouring her food. And the way her fingers hold her food just so. It's beautiful. My desk hides my hard-on.

...

Five minutes later I hear her coming. I know her voice: louder than the others, the leader of her pack. I scramble up to the chain-link fence and call her name. I've got dirt all over my knees. My face is darker in the shade of the bridge. The two other girls shriek and bolt. Stephanie calls to them but they're gone. She stands her ground. She's not scared. She checks me out, intrigued by my weird behaviour. She comes over to the fence. I must look like a prisoner, an animal in a zoo waiting to be fed.

"What tha fuck are you doing down there? Playing with yourself while the girls walk by?"

I don't know what to say to that. Like I said, Stephanie's bold, but I've got to take a chance this time.

She goes on: "It's creepy, you know. Jumping out at us girls like that. You expect to get anywhere doing this kinda weird shit?"

I open my mouth but nothing comes out. Weird shit—she's right about that. I look at her hands. She waves them around a bit, then goes, "Come on up over that fence. Get over here on this side where I can see you. It's just fuckin' weird, me talking to you through a fence."

I do what Stephanie says. I hop over and then brush the dirt and shit off my jeans.

She says, "You don't live this direction. I never seen you over here before. You're waiting for me, right? You speak at all?"

I shuffle my feet, then blurt, "You wanna go to 7-Eleven and get something to eat? A bag of chips or chocolate or something?" All I seem to think about is eating when I'm around her. And I can't help but check out her hands. Stephanie looks at me like I'm nuts. But what else can I ask? I've never been on a date; don't know how that's supposed to go. I've got nothing but loose change in my pockets. I can't take her to Swiss Chalet or Harvest Burger or to a movie. 7-Eleven is the best I can do. We could get something to eat and then split a slushy. Sounds fine by me, but Stephanie doesn't looked convinced.

"7-Eleven? Fuck. Big spender."

She does that thing where she pauses again—making me wait. It's painful, in a good way. My stomach rumbles. Stephanie looks up the street. Her friends are long gone. Something glints in her eye. She's either interested in me or just takes pleasure playing cat-and-mouse. I don't care what motivates her. So long as she goes to 7-Eleven with me.

"Okay. Best offer I've got right now. Let's go."

I can't talk. Stephanie does all the talking as we walk up to King Street to 7-Eleven. She goes on about school, about asshole teachers, men teachers who check out her ass and tits, about grade eight boys who grab her at dances, or in Strathcona Park, or at the back of the bus; wherever they can. It sounds like she's always under attack, chased by horny boys wherever she goes, that she never has any peace. I just listen. It's more educational than a full year of school.

At the store, I belly up and buy a bag of chips and a large slushy. We sit out front of the store and eat, watching the cars and buses go by on King Street. The noise makes conversation difficult. I'm fine with it. I watch Stephanie munch her chips. I don't hear properly when she asks for the slushy. I hand it to her but come up short, dropping it before she can grab it. It spills all over the place. Stephanie needs help. There's cold, blue goo all over her hands and lap. It drips off of her. Her beautiful fingers are frozen with it. She holds them in front of her, unable to shake the stuff, unable to wave her fingers around. Stephanie looks at me, distressed. I don't think, I just react. I grab her left hand and stuff two, three, four cold fingers into my mouth, sucking the slushy off of her. She looks worried, then smiles, relieved. I feel her skin warm in my mouth. I do the thumb on her left hand then follow with the thumb on her right. That leaves her four fingers on her right hand. She offers them this time. I take all four fingers into my mouth. I suck and then hold them there. I look at Stephanie. She likes this too. She leans closer into me like she wants to kiss or something. But it's not her lips I'm after right now. I've still got four of her fingers in my mouth. I bare my teeth and start to bite down.

FUCK BUDDIES

There she is again, standing outside my apartment door. I'm just home from work. I open the front door to the building, fumble with my keys, look up and BANG—it's her. More accurately, it's her ass on the landing at the top of the short flight of stairs. JUICY, it says, in sequined silver lettering about three inches high on the butt of her black sweat pants. Those pants hang down low, low enough that I see her purple G-string panties, the top hem cutting into her fleshy gunt. She's also wearing a T-shirt that looks like it would better fit a three-year-old. She's not that small; she's no petite woman. She is what it says on her ass: JUICY. If only she was *inside* my flat instead of teasing me, standing outside my door. She's my next-door neighbour. Melanie. She's in her early twenties, a couple decades younger than me. She moved in a month ago.

. . .

She was loud and in-yer-face right from the start. The first time I saw her was also coming in from work. She was leaning out the front of the building, holding the door open with one arm, screaming down the street.

"Fuck off, Paul! Don't never come back! I don't want you coming round here no more, you useless prick!"

She ignored me, or couldn't care less that I was standing watching her. She wore tiny, lime-green shorts that gave her cameltoe and a bright pink T-shirt with PORN STAR written across the chest in black letters. She was barefoot. Toenails painted black with silver sparkles. I waited for her to step back inside or acknowledge me but she just stared down the street, seething with anger.

I finally said, "Excuse me."

She glared and then barked, "The fuck you want, old man?"

I was stunned, but then fired back at her, "You kiss your mother with that mouth?"

She smiled, then said, "I haven't kissed my mother since I was, like, a kid. I do other shit with this mouth now."

I didn't doubt it. She scared me a little. I didn't want to take it any further.

"I live here," I told her.

"Good for you."

"I'd like to get by." I pointed up the stairs.

She was still straining her body to see up the street. I forced my eyes away from her tits and followed her gaze. I saw a guy a couple blocks away walking a ten-speed along the sidewalk.

"That Paul?"

She bit her lip and said, "Yeah, there he goes. Fuck sakes."

I stood a while longer, until Paul went around the corner. Only then did she really focus her attention on me. She stepped back into the building and I followed her. We stood in the small foyer, looking at each other.

"Sorry about that. It's just...well...me and Paul, like...I don't know. He's a fucker is all, and he pissed me off."

"I could tell."

"Yeah, well...Fuck it."

"Shit happens."

"Fuckin' right it does. All the fuckin' time."

Wow. Body like a portly peeler and a mouth like a sailor, I thought.

She scratched her neck with long, black-painted nails. "I'm Melanie. Mel. But I hate that name, both the long and the short of it."

I looked her up and down, took in the long and the short of her.

"I'm Steve. I live right there, apartment D. If you don't like your name, what should I call you?"

She thought that over but had no smart-assed reply. Then she said, "Guess that makes us neighbours. I just moved into C this afternoon. That fucker Paul helped me. We was supposeta celebrate after but he wouldn't even buy fuckin' pizza. I bought beer. I paid for the fuckin' cab back and forth two times bringing all my shit over. I only wanted a two-fer-fuckin'-one deal from Carnival Pizza down there on Wentworth but that cheap prick don't come up with twenty bucks to buy it."

"Bummer... You, um, brought all your furniture in a cab?"

"No, just my other shit. I don't got a lot of furniture. My brother's bringing it later. Least he says he was. He's gonna borrow a van from some dumbass friend of his or something. I got a futon, a sofa, a aquarium."

This surprised me. "You keep fish?"

She looked indignant. "Yeah. What's so fuckin' hard to believe about that?"

I didn't answer.

She went on, "And I got a TV. Least I think I do. Friend of mine said he had one for me. He's supposeta bring it over tomorrow. But that's 'cause I thought Paul was gonna fuckin' be here but that's fuckin' ruined. I could use my TV now Paul's not here."

She sounded hurt, lonely. I had to help. "Listen, it's your first day here, right? Maybe I can help out. I just came home from work. Lemme clean up and then I'll order a pizza. I'll pay for it. We can split it. Have a few of your beers. No strings attached. Just to welcome you to the building or something. We're neighbours now, right?"

She stood there unsure, surprised by my offer. She looked like she was seriously considering it but then she heard her cell phone—with a blaring, AC/DC ringtone—and bolted up the stairs into her flat. I turned and watched her go, admiring her sweet-looking ass. It filled out her shorts. She had meat on her, no question. She grabbed the phone and started yakking away, not closing the door to her place. She stood firmly in the middle of her living room, legs parted; long, brown curly hair tossed over her shoulder, looking back at me. I swear she was smiling at me; thinking what, I don't know.

...

From up on the landing, she pretends like she doesn't know it's me. It's a game she plays. She likes to act surprised to see me, even though I come home from work at 5:25 every day of the week. But I play along. I mean, look at her; of course I play along.

"You looking for something, Mel?"

"Oh! You're home…I told you not to call me that."

"Not really you didn't. You just told me you don't like your name. You never told me what to call you."

I've got a couple more steps to climb. She's above me still. She pirouettes, showing me that delicious ass of hers.

"You could call me what it says," she says, as coy and sassy as can be. "You like? They're new."

I just about blow a load right there looking at the word JUICY. I mean, fuck sakes, how do you respond to this? What do you do with a cheeky hottie who plays it to perfection? I don't do or say anything. Then I fiddle with my keys to distract myself when what I really want to do is tear her pants down and suck long and hard on her beautiful round ass.

I compose myself. "You out in the hall for a reason?"

"Yeah. I was hoping to catch you. My cell's dead. Can I borrow your phone? I don't have, like, a regular phone."

I jam the key in my door and push. "Sure. Come on in." I hold the door open to my place and she goes in before me.

"Over there. Help yourself. Local call?"

"Yeah. Thanks, Steve. I just gotta call—um—a friend."

She pauses until I realize she wants privacy. I skulk into my kitchen off the living room where the phone is. It's a small place. I'll hear her no matter where I am in the apartment. I open the fridge and take out a beer. Pop it and listen.

Thirty seconds later she calls me into the living room. "All done." She's radiant, up on her toes, a bounce in her step, her big, plump tits lively in her tight, cropped T-shirt, eyes glistening. It must have been some phone call. She's so happy she kisses me on the cheek, those big tits pressed against my left arm. I spill my beer. It froths and I turn red. She smiles like she does this sort of thing to men all the time. Then turns on her heels and is gone, saying "See ya" over her shoulder as I stare at the word JUICY on her butt.

Twenty minutes later I hear her out in the hall again. She pitter-patters down the stairs to open the building's front door. I press my eye into the peephole. I watch her let some guy in and then throw her arms around him. His hands drop to her ass right away. He gives it a good squeeze. Then she pulls her head back and they kiss, a long, sloppy, porn-style kiss, before she darts up the stairs. I watch her coming at me, getting bigger and bigger in the peephole. For a second I think she's coming right at me, like she's going to knock on my door and invite me along for whatever shenanigans she has planned. But at the last second she veers right to her place. The dude follows, of course; what man wouldn't?

I step away from the peephole and go back to my living room, TV tray, beer, and lousy meal of pasta slathered in no-name tomato sauce. I watch TV and listen in on my neighbour.

When I'm done eating, I go over to the wall that separates our two flats. I press my ear against it and hear muffled conversation.

I get a glass and listen. I hear giggling and groaning. I picture her on her hands and knees, ass in the air, while he fucks her from behind. I picture her turning round and sucking his cock, the cock that was just up her snatch. I picture her eyes looking up at him as she blows him, big tits swaying underneath her. I pull out my cock and quickly masturbate until I come, spunk dribbling onto the hardwood at my feet.

· · ·

The next few days are quiet. Mel has no visitors and I don't bump into her in the hall. Later, I see her on the street outside our building, hauling groceries and other bags out of a taxi. I offer to help but she shoos me away.

"You sure? It's no trouble."

"I gotta get these inside fast." She pushes past me, impatient. Then comes back. She leans into the backseat of the taxi to pick something up off the floor. Her right, low-cut pants ride down. Mel has a tramp stamp on her lower back of a pair of fish intertwined, one fish eating the tail of the other, while the other does the same. I admire the symmetry and then admire her ass cleavage instead. Then she's up with a clear plastic bag in her hands. Fish in water.

"Fuckin' 'scuse me, Steve," she says curtly.

In she goes with her fish. Then she's back out and quickly hands the driver a ten. She turns and looks at me. "You waitin' for something?"

I'm not. I'm just loitering, trying to make sense of her.

"'Cause you look confused. A little fucked up. You wanna come see my fish?"

In my head, I think, "No, I don't want to see your fish. What I want is to follow you up the stairs, haul you into my place, jam my face in your cunt and gnaw on your clit until you come, then flip you over, ream your ass, and fuck your shithole until I come."

But I don't say anything like that. I accept her offer to see the fish instead. We go inside. I watch her carefully transfer her new fish into the aquarium. She stares at the fish, making sure they're okay. They appear stunned for a bit but then resign themselves to the new surroundings, slowly swimming around their prison. What other choice have they got?

Mel turns to me, "You wanna get high?"

I'm still standing. The sofa she said she owned is not here. There's just the futon, which is open to a bed, in the centre of the room. Clothes lie around. A couple magazines. Fast food containers. Empty cooler, beer and booze bottles. Her cell phone is on the futon. Some shoes and boots. Stray laundry. A coffee mug. But not much else. The aquarium and the unmade futon bed dominate the room.

"Yeah, sure. Why not?"

Mel takes off. I look at the fish. They blink docilely, unaffected.

She comes back with a baggie of pot. She rolls a joint, sticks it in her mouth to moisten the paper, eyes boring into me, and then sparks it. We get high. We're both—with no other options—sitting on her futon bed. She sits cross-legged at the edge, her belly gushing over the hem of her tight pants. She's got a small aquamarine-coloured T-shirt on tight across her chest, brown hair

66

dangling down. The pot has me buzzing, my aggressive sexual urges replaced by calmer thoughts—how I'd like to stroke Mel's hair, pull off her τ-shirt, plunk her large breasts out and suck until I fall back asleep on her futon like a baby.

Her cell phone blasts a guitar riff. I try to ignore it, hoping it will stop. I'm enjoying my high too much and don't want it to end.

Mel's sharper than me. She can't ignore the phone. She grabs it. "Yeah, yeah, perfect. No, I'm not doing nothing. Just chillin' with my neighbour. Come on over. Ten minutes? Fuck. Great. I'll get ready."

Mel tosses the phone on her futon, stands and says: "I gotta take a shower, Steve. You gotta, like, go. I got someone coming over. A friend, like."

Her cunt is at eye level. Stoned, I stare at it, the hem of her panties again visible. Her pants are cut so low I think about how close I am to her vagina. I mean, it can't be more than an inch below the hem of her pants where her cunt hair starts, another inch or so down to her clit, then further to the hole: the heart of the matter. I swear I could reach up, slip a finger in the front of her pants and rub her clit without her having to open her belt. I mull this over.

Mel cuts off my reverie. "Come on, Steve. On your feet. Out ya go. Didn't know you were such a fuckin' lightweight when it comes to smoking weed."

My lips are dry and I don't speak. I take one last look at her, the fish, and then shuffle back to my place and fall asleep.

I wake an hour later, hungry. I step out to get a bite. From the corridor, I can hear Mel fucking on the futon in her living room, just on the other side of her door.

SHAG CARPET ACTION

...

And so it goes. I've come to recognize the pattern, a certain rhythm to it. Twice a week, always in the early evening, Mel has company. Then on Friday and Saturday nights she comes home from the clubs, stumbles up the stairs with some slobbering idiot at her heels, and gets fucked. Sundays she's quiet, her apartment so silent I swear I hear only the occasional burble from her aquarium. But by Monday, or, at the latest, Tuesday by six P.M. she's back on her game, letting some lout in the front door.

I start to wonder what she does for a living. Does she work at all? Her apartment's the same as mine, the mirror image. Small, one bedroom. She must pay the same rent as me: $925 a month. I can't see Henry, our cheap prick of a landlord, giving her a cut on the rent. Or maybe he does. Maybe she's got something worked out with him. I don't know. The men come and go so fast that I've stopped checking. Maybe Henry stops by for a quick shag. Or maybe she charges all her visitors. Maybe that's how she pays the rent, for the cell phone, the fish, take-out food, drugs, and booze. Maybe she's got something going on, is a savvy independent business woman, a call girl. Could be. But three or four tricks a week is not enough, right?

Then it hits me—fuck buddies, friends with benefits, boy toys. That's what's going on. Mel isn't turning tricks; she's just lonely and needy. She just likes to get it on in a no-strings-attached sorta way. She's like her fish: trapped in her flat, needy, and waiting to be fucked. But why not me? I live right next door. She could come over to my place asking for a cup of sugar or an egg and I'd be the obliging neighbour. I'd fuck her in a flash.

A few times her men have knocked on my door, getting the wrong flat. At first I just pointed to Mel's place.

"Next one over."

"Thanks, bud."

Then it started to piss me off. Why am I helping some imbecile fuck my juicy neighbour?

The next time it happened, I opened my door.

"You're not Melanie."

"Yeah, no shit."

"This is supposeta be the place."

"She moved out a month ago. In fact, I threw her out. You're outa luck, pal."

Dude looked confused. He looked over my shoulder, sniffing for the snatch he was after.

I got aggressive. "Beat it. Don't come round again. She's not here no more. GET IT?!"

He tried to talk but no words came. He shambled down the stairs, out the building's front door to the street.

It became my new routine: to intercept Melanie's dates and send them away with lies and threats. I don't know why. I mean, I like Mel. I like her a lot. And I like listening to her fuck. But I also had this sorrowful feeling about it. I started to feel like one of her fish; stuck in that aquarium, looking on wide-eyed and helpless while she fucked some dolt. I felt her slipping away, like I had some claim to her; I don't know why.

I started hanging around in the corridor like she used to, lingering by the mailboxes in the front foyer. I tried to time it right so I could bump into her on her way to the laundry room, on her way to the side of the building with her garbage. I wanted another invitation to get high, to see her fish. Her fish. This was my in—the fish. Or so I thought. I tried everything, but nothing worked. It should have been easy for me. I was deflecting her boy toys and cutting her supply. I lived next door and knew her habits, knew when she needed it.

I showed up at her door with a goldfish in a baggie on a Monday at six P.M.

"I was at the mall and saw this and thought of you."

"Cool. Urm…thanks." She took it and closed the door on me.

I went to her place with food on a Thursday at 5:55 P.M. "I was down at Carnival Pizza. They had a deal on slices. I picked one up for you."

"Cool. Urm … thanks." And then she closed the door.

Same thing with booze and drugs. She took the proffered beer or joint and then disappeared back into her flat. I got to wondering: had she gone off it? No way. She's what, twenty-two years old? No fuckin' way. Like fish, food, alcohol, and weed—sex still had to be crucial for her.

Maybe she has a rule about not fucking someone close to her. Was that it? Or maybe she changed her routine and was going out for it, instead of ordering in. Plus, I'm at work all day. Maybe she was getting it earlier in the day than before. What do I know about what she does during the day? Does she have daytime fuck buddies? Guys who work nights at bars and have nothing to do all day, afternoon shift workers from the steel plants? Or guys who work on the road—courier truck drivers, auto parts supply dudes, contractors who rove around in black pickups. Maybe even the fuckin' milkman for all I know. Too many possibilities.

Or maybe—here's a thought—it was me. I mean think about it. I'm twice her age. I could be older than her dad. Sure, she flirted with me in the early days, showing off her JUICY ass, smoking bud together—but that was ages ago.

I go into my bathroom and look in the mirror on the medicine chest. I look at my face. The lines and creases. The stubble, circles under the eyes, the start of a double chin and flabby chicken neck. I'm forty-five years old for Christ's sake. What am I thinking? I'm a middle-aged, pathetic lout living in a crappy one-bedroom apartment. I work a dull, shit job. I dress like a bum, eat bad food, and maintain bad personal hygiene habits. My best years are long gone. So a twenty-two-year-old hottie—no matter how desperate—rightly wants nothing to do with me. What a fuckin' newsflash! Wake up, old man. She was right calling you that from the start: old man. Yeah, old man, take a look at your life. I should be out chasing cougars, someone my own age. They must be out there. There must be forty-five-year-old fuck buddies. They might not be JUICY. Maybe it says SLOPPY or DROOPY on the ass of their sweatpants. No matter. I'm not juicy either. This is the long and the short of it.

I step away from the mirror. I go to my kitchen and grab a beer. Then to the front window of my apartment. I look out onto the street. An old woman pushes by with a walker. I turn away. I'm old, but I'm not geriatric. There's got to be something else.

I glance across the street at the row of decrepit townhouses adjacent to my building. Three lifelong welfare grandmothers in their mid-forties sit in lawn chairs drinking Labatt Blue surrounded by their kids' diapered rug-rats in splash pools. This is more my league.

I look down at my beer, take a drink, grab a couple of travellers, and then head for the door.

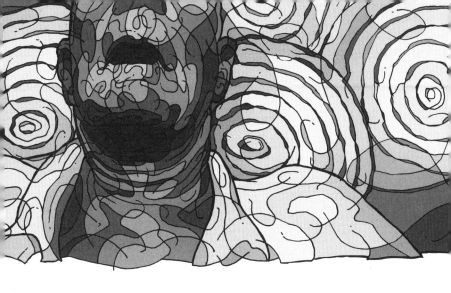

ONIONS

"Henry? Henry? What is it?"

Jason's grandma panics. His mom goes to the phone. Dad stands by grandma while all the kids stop eating, their eyes skipping off the adults.

Henry—Jason's granddad—eats whole onions cooked. His mom serves them every Sunday slathered in gravy. Henry cuts the onions in half and then pops them into his mouth, slurping when he eats. Gravy drools out sometimes. He doesn't have a lot of teeth.

Jason hears a siren. His older sister runs to the front door, his dad is right behind her. This signals Jason. He wants to leave the room, but for a moment he looks at his grandma rubbing Henry's back. Henry's head is tilted back toward the ceiling. She took off his glasses. He looks different without them. There are deep impressions on his nose and at his temples—even at this angle Jason can see that his granddad's eyes have shut, and the lids flicker weirdly, spastically.

In a farmhouse kitchen much bigger than his—Jason imagines

it from stories and old black-and-white photographs: six brothers, three sisters, no mother. She died a month after the last child was born. Two children followed her, both dying before their thirteenth birthdays. The father was a farmer on a mountain concession road. It was little more than a dirt track with rough irrigation ditches on each verge. No lights. No hydro poles. Now the site is paved with a mess of asphalt, cluttered with concrete and glass: a Wal-Mart, a Best Buy, an East Side Mario's, a giant LCBO.

His dad wedges the screen door open. The ambulance has stopped dead centre in the street. Two paramedics—just like John Gage and Roy DeSoto from Squad 51 in that old TV show *Emergency!*—bound up the steps to the house. Jason's older sister shoves him out of the way. His younger sister stares at the siren on top of the ambulance. It still emits flashing light, but has gone silent. Jason's brother bites his fingernails. His mom hurries Gage and DeSoto to the table while his grandma stands behind Henry, still rubbing his back.

"Henry. They're here. For you. Can you hear me?"

Gage goes for Henry's throat. DeSoto snaps the latches on his paramedic's case.

"He was eating?"

Mom looks horrified.

"Onions," Jason blurts.

His dad grabs Jason's left elbow and yanks back hard.

Henry never went anywhere except to work and back. Travel was unknown. It's not a word from his generation, but he did go to Saskatchewan for two years to work on a ranch when it was clear an older brother would get the family farm. He was eighteen. He

ONIONS

rode the train for a week with one small suitcase of belongings. The ranch was near the village of Livelong. Henry told Jason about it a few times when they played cribbage, how late on Saturday afternoons he'd ride a horse into town and eat at the Chinese food restaurant—which surprised Jason: a Chinese food restaurant in a tiny Saskatchewan village nearly a hundred years ago. It was also hard to imagine his granddad eating anything other than cooked onions, potatoes, and meat. Something else must have lured Henry there: a change of scenery away from the ranch and the men he worked with? A cold beer after a dusty ride into town and—who knows—maybe the restaurant owner's daughter?

"Is he going to be okay? Is he? Henry?"

Grandma still panics. Jason hears his mom's phrase:"Don't get into a panic" echo in his head. She says it whenever Jason gets too worked up. This seems like a good time to get worked up, to panic. Gage and DeSoto look annoyed. They don't like the distraction, the panicking. Jason's mom doesn't help; she doesn't follow her own advice, and panics too. Dad stays calm. He tries to keep the kids away. Above the ruckus, Jason hears a strange wheezing noise come from Henry, like his nose is stuffed and he can't breathe because he can't blow his nose because he forgot his handkerchief. He's never used Kleenex yet over the first seventy-eight years of his life and he's not about to start, even though maybe it will help him breathe and save his life. Gage hears the sound too. It's more serious than a forgotten handkerchief. Gage looks at Jason, then at DeSoto, before lunging at his case to urgently retrieve something.

Later Henry drove a truck hauling stone to Sarnia and back. Today it's maybe a two-and-a-half-hour drive. In the 1920s it was a two-day trip. The company paid for his stay at a rooming house near Point Edward. Henry got supper the day he arrived and breakfast early on the day he left. The truck was filled with a different type of stone on the return trip. Why the stone from Sarnia had to be swapped for stone from Hamilton mountain Jason has no idea. Henry made the trip three times a week for five years. Sundays he worked on his brother's farm.

Now Jason's dad is trying to calm everyone but he's having a tough time holding it together. He realizes his family might see a man die, a Sunday dinner turned horrific episode. He should really push the kids away: out to the street or to the back room to be distracted by television. But he can't herd the kids and console the two women at the same time. He is being asked to do too much.

Jason looks over and it appears DeSoto is using his granddad like a mountain; ascending Henry's chest to his neck where he attacks flesh like it's rock he needs to find purchase on. Henry's white hair flaps about from DeSoto's exertions. It looks like snow drifting on a peaceful summit.

Henry told Jason he wanted to go to Cuba, well before Castro and the Communists. He was curious about the place.

"Cuba?"

"Yes."

"Why?"

"It's a spot on a map. I liked the look of where it was. I liked the name. I thought it would be warm and it looked close enough so that it wasn't impossible. There must have been ships that could have took me there if I got east to Halifax. I remember thinking that."

"You never went?"

"No. Of course not."

"Why?"

"No money for it. And work. I went to work."

"Always?"

"Pretty much."

"No one travelled?"

"Travelled? No one I knew. Not unless wars count. That was usually a one-way trip." He laughed a little at his own joke. Then he said, "I was too young for the first war and too old for the second war. I never went nowhere that wasn't to do with work. I just thought Cuba had a nice sound to it."

Jason knows he meant nicer than a farm, the inside of a truck cab, or later, a 6:30 A.M. bus ride to a factory. Maybe Cuba was another version of the Chinese restaurant in Livelong, Saskatchewan.

"Henry? Henry! Stay with us!"

And as if this command is all he needs, and not Gage and DeSoto climbing all over him, Henry makes a sound more severe than a gurgling noise, sputters and spits, then throws his head forward into his dinner plate, his nose in the onions, goes rigid and does not move.

Gage and DeSoto look at each other.

Grandma wails "Henry! Henry! Come back to us!" Her Glaswegian accent is accentuated in her grief and torment. Jason's mom paws at his grandma. Dad looks let down by the uniformed men in his house. Kids cower and wait for blame to be served. Onions? Was it onions? Or old prairie dust caught in his throat sixty years ago that finally cut off his breathing? Some toxic industrial workplace substance resurrected decades later that brought him down? Foolish dreams of a restaurant waitress or Cuba? No—the obituary will mention none of these things. In fact, it doesn't. Jason reads it online from a back issue of the *Hamilton Spectator*. The insipid phrase "Quietly at home" is used. Bullshit, Jason thinks. He was there. He heard the strange noises his granddad made and how his grandma hollered—there was nothing quiet about it. Jason heard the sound of Henry's face squelching in onions. After that he never breathed again. Henry was quiet at that point but not before. The rest of it says the usual about being survived by "loved ones"—this is true, but cliché. It mentions Henry's years working at Firestone and the Otis elevator factory; always important details to bring out old-timers and representatives from the union Locals. It gives information on the funeral home visitation and the burial ceremony. But that's it. Just words: a man's life thinned with no mention of onions. Cooked onions. Henry ate cooked onions whole. Someone should have at least mentioned that.

THE ROOKIE AND THE WHORE

We call him the Rookie because that is what he is. It is not the most original nickname. We are Senior A lacrosse players in a shitkicker Ontario town. We are not lawyers or doctors.

Stumpy, G, Tex, Dewey—the rest don't have nicknames. There was a guy who played a couple seasons ago we called The Messiah. I don't know who came up with that. It wasn't me. It was likely one of the out-of-towners. Some of them go to university in the off-season while the rest of us work.

It is close to four o'clock in the morning back at the hotel. The Rookie runs around the hotel room with a bottle of wine in one hand. He wears nothing but sports socks. His dick bounces and jostles. Not that I'm looking.

We played earlier tonight against Orangeville and won 12-10. We had them down 10-4 going into the third period, but Turk Henderson scored three quick goals and made it a game. We had to turn it back on. All that hard work made the beers go down nicely afterward.

The Rookie was all smiles after the game. He scored his first goal in Senior. It only took him eight games. He has no hands. Anyone can see that. But he has a big heart. He also dropped the gloves with one of the Hoyle brothers, which wasn't the smartest move. The Rookie got the first punch in. That just woke Hoyle up. But the Rookie came back later and scored. Then, even later, at Brothers Bar and Grill, the deep cut under the Rookie's left eye drew the attention of a couple of locals. The Rookie can't dance, much like he can't fight. The women soon gave up on him. So the Rookie fell back on a sure thing: Broom Hilda.

Tex calls to him, "Hey, Rookie, get over here. Broom Hilda needs another cock."

Tex sits on the edge of the bed slowly jerking off. He reaches over and slaps Broom Hilda's ass. G fucks her from behind. She's on all fours, with her face mashed in a pillow. The Rookie comes over. He tugs his cock to get it hard.

"Fuck her in the ass?" he pants.

Tex laughs. "Fuck. No. Leave that to G. He's going back and forth. Put it in her mouth."

Broom Hilda pops her head up. She's not pretty but she has a great body. She looks at the Rookie and slurs, "Bring it on, Rookie. Do your worst."

The Rookie titters and goes to the end of the bed. Tex gets up. He stands over the scene like he's directing porn. "That's it, G. Fuck that cunt. Rook, get your cock in her mouth. That's it. Faster, Rookie. Yeah, fuck her mouth fast, fuck like a rabbit." Tex laughs. "The Rookie and the Whore. Like the Rabbit and the Hare. Fuck that mouth, Rookie. See how long you can last!"

80

THE ROOKIE AND THE WHORE

The Rookie does what he's told. Broom Hilda makes a gargling noise—half gagging, half lustful moaning. The Rookie is not going to last long.

And then I think about what Tex said. It was the tortoise and the hare, not the rabbit and the hare. A rabbit *is* a hare. Tex has it all wrong, but he laughs and laughs anyway.

Broom Hilda is also a nickname. Her real name is Miranda. She is the younger sister of Kent, the stick guy in the John Deere cap. Kent never says much. You throw him your stick and he fixes it. His sister is the town whore, a real team player. Senior A lacrosse players all summer; Junior A hockey players all winter.

I stay away. I'm a married man and I have to live in this town. I don't just drive up from down south for the weekend to play lacrosse and party. I drink and do some coke. But I don't put my cock anywhere near Broom Hilda.

I look over at the bed. The Rookie cums and falls back. He still has the bottle in his hand. Red wine sloshes on the carpet. His dick smears against his thigh. He's passed out. Tex laughs. But now his cock is hard, so he takes the Rookie's place. Broom Hilda blows him. He cums. Then G pulls out and cums on her ass. I watch. The race is over and the Rookie is done while the whore carries on. So it's a bit like that old story after all.

Behind Tex, G, and Broom Hilda, Stan and Billy snort lines of coke off a bedside table. Pete and Dewey slouch in the hotel room's doorframe, sharing a joint. I sit in a chair by the window. Outside, the town is pretty much dead quiet. There is the odd squeal of tires or party howl. It is very late and I should go home or I'll end up passed out like the Rookie.

I stand at the exact moment that Broom Hilda looks up. My movement catches her eye. She looks at me and I step back. To be honest, she scares the shit out of me. She smirks and heads to the bathroom to wash out her mouth and clean the cum-smear off her ass. Stan and Billy finish their lines and watch her pass. She'll be back. Stan and Billy strip down to their gitch and stand by the bed, waiting, jangling their cocks so they'll be ready. Tex and G move away and stagger back to their hotel room to get four hours sleep before practice tomorrow.

Billy sees the Rookie lying on the carpet. He snickers and walks over. He squats and farts. Pete and Dewey—shitfaced and stoned—laugh. I can't help but laugh. The Rookie rubs his nose like a fly has landed on him. I step past and try to leave, but Pete holds a joint out to me. I take a drag. Then Broom Hilda comes out of the can. Again she assesses me and asks with her eyes when I'm going to take my turn. She must think I'm queer or pussy-whipped or both. She can't understand why someone on this team would pass her up. Maybe one day I'll explain it to her. But not now. Now I want to leave, but the weed feels pretty good. I slump down in the door-frame with Pete and Dewey. Broom Hilda goes past, bare-assed and proud. Stan grabs her and throws her on the bed. She laughs, coos, then lies back and spreads her legs. The last thing I see before passing out is her black-haired gash puckered and ready for all comers.

• • •

The Rookie is a sloppy, bumbling idiot the next day at practice. He's a pup, after all. He hasn't learned how to party and still function the day after. He trips stepping onto the floor. The Rookie can't catch a ball. They bounce off his shoulders, his helmet; one hits him in the throat. At a break, about six guys throw balls at him at once. The Rookie falls down in defeat, which only leads to more balls thrown at him. But he toughs it out. He doesn't leave the floor. He doesn't vomit, which is something. When the practice is over, the coach makes the Rookie run stairs. Booze pours out in the Rookie's sweat.

Stories fly when the Rookie comes into the dressing room. Everything is exaggerated. But by noon everyone is showered and relatively sober. The coach calls a brief meeting. I sit across the room from the Rookie. His eyes are glazed and he looks worried. Someone told him Broom Hilda passed him a dose, and he can't remember what he did, or where he stuck his cock, so he believes it.

Later, in the parking lot outside the arena, Gordie cracks a case of Canadian. Day-after beers are supped slowly. The half of the team that smokes lights up. The sun beats down on us. Slowly, we gather steam. The case of beer is emptied. Coolers with more beer and sandwiches appear. It's Sunday afternoon and we're all getting an easy buzz on after practice.

Broom Hilda talk starts again. The Rookie squirms, but also looks more confident now. Then it's five o'clock. The out-of-towners go to their cars. The townies linger, not having to be anywhere. I haven't seen the wife in more than twenty-four hours but neither have any of the townies. That can wait, like tomorrow's workday. We crack more beers. A bottle of whisky comes out. Joints are sparked. We wave goodbye to the out-of-towners as they head for Highway Six and the long drives back to Toronto, Hamilton, and Ohsweken. A last few catcalls are thrown at the Rookie. But he'll be back next weekend to take another run at Broom Hilda. Me—I'll stay clear and let the Rookie have his fun while he can. He won't be a rookie forever.

DOG FUCKER BLUES

Lenny Lazaruscu shakes his head in disgust. The two guys he works with on the KP crew stand by a pothole, leaning on their shovels. They're yakking away. Not doing a shred of work. Fucking the dog in a big a way.

It's not the dog-fucking that bothers Lenny. As a faithful and long-time City employee, Lenny knows you shouldn't kill the job and that everyone should *pace* themselves at work. But it has to be within reason.

Lenny is pissed off with how his co-workers talk. Buddy One—Lenny doesn't remember his name; he's a new guy who was just assigned to Lenny's truck this morning—says to Buddy Two, whose name Lenny does know (Anton), "I fuckin' just don't fuckin' see why we're rocking the boat is all. Like what the fuck? I don't go to the meetings or nothing but like what the fuck is the union leadership getting so fuckin' jacked up about?"

Anton leans on his shovel like Ken Dryden on a goalie stick. He says to Buddy One, "Agree with you there a hundred per cent,

85

dude. The fuckin' union is out to fuckin' lunch. Don't know their assholes from this here pothole."

Anton gestures with his right steel-toed boot at the pothole and they both get a good laugh out of it. Anton is *hilarious*. Then he goes on, "I got no use for the fuckin' union neither. Let us work, get our fuckin' cheques, get pissed and go see the rippers. Know what I'm saying?"

Buddy One perks up at the mention of every city worker's two main interests: drinking and strippers. Not to be outdone by Anton, he fires back: "Fuckin' right! I know exactly what you mean. I hooked up with a couple dudes from garbage down at Hanrahan's last week. Bought some blow off the one fucker. Then we really partied. Turns out one of them garbage guys…fuck, what was his name?" Buddy One actually scratches his greasy-haired head with a grubby, gloved hand. Then he continues: "Dupre…Dupont or something…"

Anton lights up. "Fuck! You mean Duguay! You really partied with Duguay? That fucker is a fuckin' legend!"

Buddy One points the butt end of his shovel in Anton's direction. "Yeah, that's the dude's name! Big fucker. Biker moustache. Crazy son of a bitch."

Lenny cringes when he hears Duguay's name. He knows where this story is going: straight to Hell. He looks around the quiet street. He's mildly concerned that their dog fucking is carrying on too long. That and Lenny's pissed that the greenhorn labourer spouts anti-union crap and talks about partying with Duguay all at the same time. It really rankles Lenny. But he also wants to hear more and suss out where—aside from Hell—the conversation between the two simpletons with shovels is going. Lenny stands a step or two behind them by the truck's hot box.

Now Buddy One starts getting really worked up, like he's high on coke again. "That Duguay fucker. What an animal! We pounded the beers all night, eh. Shots of rye and tequila. Blow. Turns out he knows some of them peelers, right. Fuck sakes!"

Anton leans forward on his shovel, hanging on every word.

"Duguay was with a couple other guys from garbage. And some real bikers. Red Diamonds from down on the beach strip. You know their place. Well, when the fuckin' ripper joint closes officially, like, we all have a private fuckin' party. Duguay lets me hang around once he finds out I'm city. Fuckin' ace of spades! Fuck the lap dances and that shit: after some lines, these two peelers do a live fuckin' sex show for us. There was maybe six or seven of us watching, right."

Lenny inches closer, away from the heat.

Anton practically humps his shovel handle.

Buddy One is scoring major points. He goes on: "They was like rubbing up against each other, clam bashing. Their cooches was all shaved or waxed or whatever the fuck. Holy fuck, man. Then the bikers start fuckin' 'em, like gangbang style. I didn't know what the fuck, I was so fuckin' baked and all. Then Duguay and his buddies get blow jobs. Duguay gives me the nod and this one ripper, a real fuckin' hottie with huge jugs, she comes over to blow me, but Duguay stepped in first."

Buddy One pauses for effect. Anton can't take it. He's about to knock a load off in his workpants. Lenny eyeballs the neighbourhood. No one around. The hot box simmers and hisses behind him.

Buddy One continues his story: "Duguay tells me I get a blow job *only* if I voted *against* the fuckin' strike. For a second, I was fuckin' like: 'Did I hear you right?' But then I looked at the fucker and could tell he meant fuckin' business. I tells him: 'Yeah, of course I fuckin' voted against the strike.' I mean, I never went to that meeting or nothing but I wanted that bitch to suck my cock big time. So then he just smiles. My word was fuckin' good enough for him, eh. Fuckin' ace of spades! Then he snaps his fingers and the ripper carries on. She goes down to her knees and sucks me off right there in the bar while Duguay looks on, smiling like an evil fucker." Buddy One is sweating now. He wipes his brow with the cuff of his right work glove and pauses again.

Anton can't take it. He spurts: "That the end? Fuck sakes!"

Lenny peers at the new guy. Telling the story looks like it has sapped all his energy.

Then Buddy One comes back to life and offers a debauched conclusion: "I thought for a fuckin' sec I wouldn't be able to get it on with Duguay fuckin' looking at me like that. So I concentrated real hard on the ripper. She was fuckin' good at it, of course. I stared at her pretty brunette head bobbing on the end of my knob. I wanted to give her a facial but I figured that'd be offside or some shit. So I came hard in her sweaty little mouth. Fuck, what a fuckin' night…"

They all stand there, unsure what to do next. Buddy One is spent. Anton looks torn between being jealous and proclaiming that Buddy One is his new personal god.

Finally, Lenny breaks the silence: "Well, we know who owns your ass now then, don't we, son?"

Buddy One and Anton startle, like they forgot Lenny was there. Anton steps away from Lenny a bit and stumbles into the pothole. He rights himself and looks over at the older man. "The fuck you mean by that, Len?"

"I just mean our new friend here pretty much sold his ass to Duguay for the price of a blow job. That's what I mean."

Anton doesn't get it.

Buddy One tenses and turns on Lenny. "The fuck you on about?"

Lenny steps forward. Like Duguay, he's also a big man, though a decade older than Duguay and probably twenty years older than the rookie. He looks down at Buddy One: "What's your name again, son?"

"Wally. It's fuckin' Wally."

"Wally fuckin' what?"

"Wally fuckin' Wozniewski."

"Well, Brother Wozniewski, here's what it means. Duguay never does nothing without a purpose. He don't give up his drugs to people and let them get their little cocks sucked by some whore at Hanrahan's for no reason at all. That party you had; it was your soul you sold to Duguay, all for the price of some coke and a lousy blow job."

Wally doesn't say anything.

Then Anton comes to Wally's defence: "No such thing as a *lousy* blow job, Len." He's trying to be funny again—to break the tension—but it doesn't work.

Wally looks perplexed, even more than usual. You can practically hear the gears turn in his head. Finally he comes up with something: "What the fuck does Duguay want with me? What good am I to him?"

Lenny says, "Don't undervalue yourself, son. Duguay is all about drugs and where and who to sell them to across this vast city." Lenny sweeps an arm around like a priest delivering a sermon. And it is a sermon of sorts. Both Wally and Anton look at the older man, taken in by his wisdom.

Lenny carries on: "Duguay is partnered with the bikers. Now that he's got you, you can expect him to come to you for some payback. A returning of the favour, as it were. At the very least, you'll become a regular paying drug customer. Or he'll force you to send buyers his way. Or, you remember his question about the strike vote? Well, he'll have you work the rank and file to help him divide and conquer the bargaining unit. Just don't let him find out you were bullshitting about being at the vote. Understand? Duguay's new purpose these days is to fuck up the membership and end the possibility of a strike, since the vote didn't turn out the way he wanted. You getting any of this?"

Lenny is pretty sure the imbecile still doesn't understand. Anton doesn't.

Wally rubs his nuts with a gloved hand. A cold look passes across his face. Then he turns away from Lenny, tightens his grip on his shovel and suddenly seems *really* interested in the pothole in front of him. Wally says—eyes turned away from both Lenny and Anton—"Shouldn't we get some fuckin' work done before the white hats show up?"

Anton hoists his shovel. Lenny snorts and shakes his head again. Then he steps back to the hot box and throws open the hopper. The acrid stench of asphalt assaults the air. Wally and Anton dig their shovels into the warm bitumen and start filling the black hole blacker.

* * *

Here's the situation: Negotiations are going south. That's putting it mildly. They're at a bloody impasse. They're logjammed. Plugged and backed-up. Negotiations are simply going nowhere fucking fast and a strike deadline looms heavy.

The union is divided. That's an oxymoron: union, divided. And I know what you're thinking: oxymoron is a big word for a Class 3 truck driver/general labourer like me, Lenny Lazaruscu. But I'm no idiot. I know a few words longer than one syllable. I'm no moron, either. Not like half the dolts I work with. They can't grasp that the employer wants us divided because it makes it *so* much easier for them to stuff their agreement down our throats. Half the assholes I work with have never heard the word *solidarity*, never mind know what it means. That's the problem nowadays. They only understand and care about one-syllable words, words like pay, beer, weed, and cunt. Fancy, meaningful words like *solidarity* are lost on them. Which means the employer has us by the balls. But it's not like the employer is sitting too pretty, either. The taxpayer associations are making their usual stink about pissing away public money to pay inflated city-worker salaries. The mayor crows about how the city's hands are tied having to rely on property tax income for revenue. The mayor says the union has to see that we're living in a new fiscal reality now. And so the city's negotiating team is putting the boots to the union. The public is not sympathetic. Unemployment runs close to twelve per cent in this town. We're seen as fat cats with secure, slack jobs, while so many others bust their balls for minimum wage or live hand to mouth on EI, welfare or under-the-table work. We're in a bad way, no question.

It doesn't help that we're not putting up a united front. The young guys just don't get it. They don't know or care about the history of the Local and the battles it fought and won to get them what they've got now. They just moan about union dues coming off their cheques and say stupid things like we should decertify. Except that's too big a word for them. What they actually say is something like: "Who needs the fuckin' union anyway. What's it ever fuckin' done for me?"

And then there are the ethnic divisions. The Italians don't want trouble. They just want to keep their heads down, mix and spread their fucking cement, and then go home to tend their grapes and tomatoes. The Portuguese want a strike. They want the summer off, probably because they want to spend even more time tending their grapes and tomatoes, that and playing cards at their "social clubs" up on James Street North. The Serbs and Croatians are on either side of the issue—big fucking surprise, that. The Poles I can't read, except for that dolt Wozniewski, who is clearly dumb as a stump. Anton is Czech or Slovenian or some fucking thing, which means, like me, he doesn't even register on the ethnicity scale.

Then there are the newer immigrant groups. They're all over the map. I worked with a Sri Lankan labourer last week. He said he's against the strike because there is no way his family can survive on strike pay and the shitty wages his wife makes at a laundromat. I worked with a Vietnamese dude just the other day and he was *all* for the strike. He spouted union propaganda like he was straight out of the Labour College. Turns out, after a little asking around, I learned he won a scholarship and spent a week in Toronto at a course put on by national called "Leadership in the Union." It was scary how well rehearsed his message sounded but at least he's on the right side of the issue.

Then there are the guys with criminal connections. Take Duguay, the insane garbageman that every city worker knows or has heard about. He's tight with the Red Diamonds motorcycle club. You've likely heard that garbage—er, "waste management"— and organized crime go hand in hand. I'll leave it at that. Plus the Red Diamonds sell drugs to half the workers and a healthy percentage of city management as well. A strike would hurt their business. You can't buy much weed, coke, speed, crystal meth, OxyContin, or junk on strike pay. The whole thing now is like the former USSR: a little external pressure mixed with internal turmoil and the entire union splinters along ethnic and economic lines.

Plus the foremen have been having their fun, shifting us around like we're circus animals playing musical chairs. You show up to work and immediately you're told to report somewhere else. Garbage guys are sent off to the Districts. Districts guys go to the cemeteries. Golf course workers to the arenas and rec centres. They send us everywhere but the mayor's fucking office. And we don't spend more than a couple days in the same job, further fracturing our solidarity. Misinformation runs rampant. Rumours spread. Bullshit flies in every direction. Sure, we grieve the job shuffling, but the union is too busy fighting at the bargaining table. It has no resources to deal with our grievances. The city is laughing and we've got less than forty-eight hours to resolve this before our strike deadline. Trouble is, the union is so weak that our strike threat packs no punch.

The issues: job cutbacks and privatization. But the city spews crap about wages when it steps away from the table into press scrums. Wages always gives the media a hard-on. There's nothing like a cliché headline about overpaid civil servants to get the readership in a flap. Letters to the editor pour in and get increasingly bitter. Mad dogs call in to radio phone-in shows and stop just short of demanding public executions for city workers.

"They should consider themselves lucky to have a job, the lazy louts. In my job, we work a full day, take pride in it and take what the bosses give us. Fire the lot of them if they don't want to work. They're not going to hold the public hostage with their selfish demands. Lazy, lazy, lazy."

That's quoted directly from a letter to the editor. I read it this morning in the *Spectator*. I recognize the name of the irate citizen. It's my next-door neighbour, Kevin Sakamoto, a guy in the Steelworkers Union who makes 80K a year and gets six weeks holidays after twenty-five years on the job. Plus he gets an extra month off when the plant shuts down every August to re-tool. He's one to talk. Now I sound bitter, like I'm taking sides and lashing out at the wrong people. You'd think in this lunch-bucket town our fellow brothers and sisters in other unions would support us and show a little solidarity. Ah, there's that word again. Maybe I'm just a dinosaur, believing workers should stand together. We'll see tonight at the emergency membership meeting called by the Local.

• • •

The first person Lenny sees when he steps off the escalator on his way to the meeting in the Hamilton Convention Centre is Duguay. He's positioned himself with a bunch of his grunts right where anyone and everyone going to the meeting has to run his gauntlet.

Duguay steps towards Lenny. "Evening, Brother Lazaruscu."

He knows what side of the strike Lenny is on. His false show of solidarity—invoking the "brother" greeting—is meant to be ironic. Duguay is a criminal who swings between pothead and cokehead as it suits his moods, but he understands irony. He could likely define it for you, if you asked. Like Lenny said, the public might regard city workers as idiots, but they're smarter than they look, especially Duguay. Lenny doesn't take his bait.

"Evening to you, Brother Duguay," he snaps back.

One of Duguay's muscleheads steps in front of Lenny, blocking his path to the meeting. The big man speaks: "We'd like you to reconsider your position on the strike, brother. We fear you haven't thought the matter through completely. That you simply haven't considered all the facets and ramifications."

Lenny is partly stunned at the language. The guy still in his filthy green city worker clothes and bright orange fluorescent T-shirt, with four days' growth on his face, looks like he should be riding with the Red Diamonds. And maybe he does, after hours or on weekends. But he comes across sounding like a businessman talking corporate-speak. This is the new reality. But Lenny is not shy. He doesn't back down easily. What the hooligan fails to realize—the ramification *he* fails to consider—is that Lenny is really on his side. Lenny is looking out for him. Lenny is all about saving the jobs the workers still have at the city and preserving Duguay and his posse's clientele. The Neanderthal doesn't know it or can't be bothered to find out.

So Lenny tells him this: "Listen, brother…what's your name again? We've never worked together. I'd remember you."

"Lewis. Brother Lewis."

He doesn't offer his hand.

"Okay. Brother Lewis. Here's the thing: I pretty much know all the facets of this possible strike. I've studied it from every angle. It keeps me up at night, thinking about it. I've actually got a long-term view of the matter. The way I see it, I don't just want to keep your job for the sake of keeping it, or Duguay's there, or any of your jobs. I want to keep all of us working. It'd be good for you guys and your—ahem—business, if you follow me."

Lewis looks sideways at Lenny. He chews on Lenny's words, trying to take it all in and follow where Lenny leads him.

Lenny starts again: "Here's a ramification maybe you haven't considered. Let's say the city gets its way and we lose a couple hundred jobs or they contract out our work to a private company. Do you think that private company will pay us anything close to what we're getting now? Do you think if that happens that the stooges left behind scraping by on shitty pay will have any money leftover for recreational pursuits, particularly like you provide?

and ramifications and not just the short-term gain."

Lenny tries to step around Lewis. Lewis is clearly bamboozled by Lenny's speech.

Duguay, however, has been listening closely. He's not impressed. He's well and truly pissed. He steps in.

"Listen, fuckwad!"

"What happened to 'Brother Lazaruscu'?"

"Fuck that shit, asshole. Listen, and listen good, you wise-assed Italian fucker!"

Lenny snaps, "'Lazaruscu' is hardly an Italian name, you ignoramus. It's Romanian!"

"Whatever the fuck. You're a greaseball like the rest of them fuckers as far as I can fuckin' tell!"

Duguay is back to sounding like a moron. That, and he's practically frothing at the mouth.

"This strike ain't gonna happen! I'll make sure of that!"

He steps closer to Lenny, trying to intimidate him. Lenny doesn't back down.

"You realize you're too late for that, right?" Lenny says.

Duguay snarls.

Lenny goes on, "I mean, where were you guys when we had the strike vote? Ninety-three per cent in favour. You know the results. I don't have to tell you. You shoulda done your lobbying a long time ago. Too fuckin' late now."

Duguay is about to explode. His face turns red and he reaches for Lenny's neck but right then the Local president, Larry Marshall, cuts in.

"Hey, hey," Marshall spits—almost literally; he has a terrible lisp. "We're union brothers. Brother Duguay, you best take your hands off Brother Lazaruscu."

Marshall signals over two of the Local executive—Mert Signarsson and Dom Lujic. They rival Duguay and his thugs in size. Signarsson puts a large hand on Duguay's shoulder. Duguay eyeballs him, looks at his men; maybe thinks about staying out of jail and staying employed. He backs away from Lenny, but not without a warning.

"It's not over. This fuckin' strike, if it happens, will not end pretty."

Marshall tries to make nice. "Brother Duguay, you have to respect the democratic process. You had your chance to vote and you weren't at the meeting. The membership has spoken. If negotiations continue the way they are, we're walking and everyone will have to support that move. Let's not let the employer see us bicker like little kids. Let's stay united."

Marshall is about to launch into a full speech by the sounds of it when Lujic steps in. "Larry. Meeting needs to start."

"Right. Let's all go to the meeting where we will each have a chance to be heard. It's the honoured tradition of trade unionism."

Now even Lenny wants to puke. Marshall lays it on too thick. No good politician. But he has defused the situation. Duguay and his posse skulk away. Marshall nods arrogantly to his disciples. Lenny composes himself. The small crowd of onlookers disperses and they all head inside the huge meeting room.

...

Lenny has put in twenty-six years with the city. He came on the job when he was eighteen. He was straight out of grade twelve, which makes him more educated than his average co-worker. It shows, when you think of Wally and Anton, for example.

Lenny has worked all over the city in many departments and jobs. He was hired first as a general labourer and started on the weed crew, which is easily the worst job in the city. Then it was the crack-sealing crew, which is not as much fun as the name suggests. Then the cement-framing crew, where at least there Lenny bonded a little with the Italians, although they still looked down their noses at him, as if he was some sort of distant barbarian cousin, being Romanian. Next it was the road saw, but that just did in Lenny's hearing. Lenny spent some time on garbage, where he first clashed with Duguay. He tried working in the arenas, but that was too slow, even for a city worker. Although it was a chance to hang around hockey moms and get free beer by letting the pick-up guys drink in the dressing rooms late at night. Cemeteries—yes, even slower than arenas, and far less female talent on display. Then Lenny worked on one of the city's municipal golf courses. That was when he put in to become a Districts driver. Dealing with assholes on the municipal course who thought they were nouveau riche private-course snobs was too much. Lenny once chased a golfer in a cart while brandishing a hard rake over his head like a battle-axe. That was the last straw. The city tried to fire him. But he was only suspended two weeks with pay, thanks to the union stepping in to save his ass.

SHAG CARPET ACTION

Lenny had fifteen year's seniority at that point. He got his driver's class license and moved back to public works. He's been a KP driver ever since. KP stands for "cold patch." Nobody knows why it's not called "CP." Lenny just goes with it. With some guys it's still called "hot box." This again is a misnomer, because the bitumen is supposed to be warm. It's air temperature when it goes in the box and is then heated a little to keep it loose. They stopped calling the crew "hot box" when the yard took on three women labourers. Turns out one of them got offended when some jughead started giggling and saying idiot, adolescent things about her *hot box*. The union was called in. The jughead in question was sent to a weekend equality workshop. He came back reformed, sort of. The woman got her wish and the crew officially dropped the "hot box" moniker. Although, looking at her, there was little chance anyone would confuse her for a hottie—an Estonian shot-putter, maybe.

Lenny has worked with dozens of guys over the years. Anton is the most steady. Others come and go. It's among the simplest of city jobs. Each morning Lenny is given a list of twelve to fifteen jobs. It's all small patch work around the city; filling potholes on streets and smoothing out trips on buckled sidewalks, all with material left over by the asphalt crew.

Lenny is also the lead hand. He takes job orders from the foreman. He gets the truck ready and drives it. He decides the pace, when to go for coffee and dinner. Anton, and whoever else ends up on the truck, are the grunts. They set up cones to establish a safe work space on the road. They shovel the KP; spread it and smooth it. Lenny inspects their work and decides when a hole needs less or more bitumen. When it rains too much they sit in the truck.

When it snows too much they drive more and try to stay invisible. If it's too wintery and cold, even for KP, Lenny tinkers and cleans the truck while Anton and whoever get reassigned for a few days shovelling snow or some other useless shit job.

When spring comes the roads are a mess. But KP patches are a short-term solution. Lenny has to deal with the public. Often, at first, citizens are happy to see the truck on their street. They smell asphalt and think they're getting a brand new tarmac. When it turns out to be a rough patch job with gluey, cold bitumen spread by a couple of monkeys with battered old shovels; the citizens are less than impressed. This is when Lenny has to bear their tirades that usually go something like:"I pay my taxes like everyone else in this stupid city. Why don't they fix my street proper? I'll tell you why: this is a working-class neighbourhood and City Hall doesn't give a rat's dirty asshole about us. They just take care of all the fat cat fuckers in the west end and on the mountain."

Lenny agrees with them. Lenny lives on a shitty working-class street, too, on Hughson Street, down by Barton. He lives walking distance to the District #2 Public Works yard on Ferguson, just north of Barton, by the old jail. He knows the complaining citizens have legit beefs but he also knows things will never change; that is, unless the union can practise what it preaches and create a workers' utopia.

Lenny's been active in the Local for a long time, although he's stopped short of running for elected office. Lenny hates politicians, whether union or the City Hall types or even the Prime Minister. Lenny believes in the power of the working man as a collective. He never misses a Local 689 meeting. No matter the weather or whatever the hell might be on television, Lenny is there every third Thursday of the month (minus July and August, of course, when union business grinds to a halt for summer) at the rundown Local 689 Hall at the end of Catharine Street North. There have been meetings when Lenny is just about the only rank-and-file member present. The Executive out-numbering regular members at a meeting is embarrassing but a reality a lot of the time. The Local boasts over eight-hundred members. The vast majority have no use for union meetings, not when they can be out getting pissed, chasing skirt, or sitting at home surrounded by their brood, nursing a twelve of Lakeport Dry, watching hockey or football on TV. It's a sad state of affairs and enough to make Karl Marx roll over in his grave.

But once the noose tightened on negotiations, the union hall started to fill up. Members were concerned. Rumours flew about a strike. About layoffs. About contracting out jobs. An extra meeting was added on the first Thursday of each month for four months running, while the bargaining unit watched its collective agreement expire and no new contract come in to take its place. Eventually, the Local hall was too small. Lenny brimmed with pride at the sight of all his union brothers and sisters putting aside other distractions to focus on solidarity. But it soon became clear there was little unity within the Local. The longer they worked without a contract, the more heated the meetings became and the more the speeches from the floor took on a nasty tone. Irate members filibustered and ranted, trying to keep dissenting opinion from being heard. The Executive struggled to keep it all under control. Small acts of intimidation and violence occurred when the meetings let out. Broken noses and black eyes became common. One dude from cemeteries had his arm broken. Side campaigns were run. Members chose sides. Soon the meetings had to be moved to the convention centre downtown to accommodate everyone. That's when the media took notice. But the Executive made sure the doors were barred and that only card-carrying members of Local 689 were allowed in.

Eventually, some of the steam came out and fewer members started turning up when they grew tired of listening to long-winded diatribes. The Local retreated back to the hall in the North End. The bargaining unit continued to work without a contract month after month. And then it happened: a motion was made from the floor that the Local needed to stop fucking around; to shit or get off the pot and call for a strike or accept the city's diluted extension of the old contract. Bang, just like that. The Executive scrambled, wanted to stall, but agitation from the floor grew. Marshall decreed a strike vote would be called in a week.

Posters were printed. Emails sent. The Local put some shit up on its shitty website. Still, less than half the membership turned out to vote and the motion to strike passed by a landslide because it was only the small, hardcore faction—that included Lenny—who was paying attention. The rest, like Duguay, had stopped paying attention months ago. They were back to smoking weed and getting blow jobs from peelers in the parking lot outside Hanrahan's. This is where it stands now.

• • •

Inside the huge convention centre meeting room, Larry Marshall ambles to a speaker's podium at the front of the room. Signarsson and Lujic stand beside him—one on his right hand and one on his left hand. Marshall taps the mic with an index finger. Feedback squelches through the room.

The president lisps: "This thing fuckin' workin'?"

Someone hollers from the middle of the room: "Of course it is, Larry! Carry on, Brother! Let's get down to business!"

Signarsson and Lujic instinctively tense and scan the crowd.

Someone else shouts, "Let the President speak. This is urgent shit."

"Shut the fuck up! You're just wasting fuckin' time your own self!" This comes from somewhere among the sea of mostly men in green work clothes.

This brings Duguay to his feet. He's not shy. He wants everyone to know he's speaking. "Everyone just calm the fuck down and let's get down to fuckin' business here."

A brave, smartass dissenter chirps, "Yeah, we know all about you and your business, Brother Duguay."

Signarsson takes a step toward the crowd. But Marshall puts a hand on Signarsson's shoulder and yanks back on his leashed pit bull. Away from the mic he says, "It's harmless, Mert. Let 'em get it out of their systems."

More bullshit banter follows. Duguay doesn't sit down. He makes obscene gestures. There is laughter. More swearing. Marshall endures it for two minutes or so and then starts tapping on the mic with a black magic marker as thick as a dildo. It takes a while but the crowd quiets enough.

Marshall holds his hands up like the messiah and starts talking. "Brothers and sisters, our backs are against the wall. Yes, things are urgent. By rights, we could be on strike in less than forty-eight hours."

He pauses and then steps over to a flipchart. He writes "48 HOURS" with the black magic marker. It has some sort of effect, as there are no more catcalls from the crowd. Flipcharts tend to mesmerize trade unionists. Marshall learned this a long time ago.

Marshall goes on: "That's right, forty-eight hours. That's not a lot of time. But maybe there is another way. A way to buy us some more time. I know we have a strike mandate, but something tells me the full heart of the union is not behind taking action. Something tells me it's a weak mandate, not a full and pure mandate."

Marshall pauses again. This time there is shuffling, grumbling, and muttering in the meeting room.

The president carries on. "The Executive met"—here he nods at Signarsson and Lujic—"and examined the possibilities. We looked through our bylaws closely, because this is important shit we're dealing with. And here's what we found."

Marshall goes over to the flipchart again. He tears off the top sheet and hands it to Signarsson. Mert tapes it to the wall behind them. Marshall stands poised over a clean sheet of flipchart paper. Then he writes "43.2." He steps back and points at it with the dildo-sized marker. Marshall says: "That number mean anything to anyone?"

Some dumbass hollers out: "That a reference to the Bible? We in shit that deep we gotta start calling on the Lord to bail us out?"

This gets some laughter from the idiot crew. But most of the members are confused and concerned, so they stare at the "43.2" and don't say anything.

Finally, Duguay stands up. "Let me hazard a guess, Larry. That number refers to a certain bylaw in our Local's constitution, right?"

Duguay keeps standing.

Marshall points the phallic marker at him: "Bingo. We have a winner!"

Stupid laughter follows. But Duguay doesn't laugh. He goes on: "That bylaw, if memory serves me right, says something about reversing a motion to strike, right Larry? That motion says something about declaring a motion to strike null and void if certain stipulations for a full and accurate strike vote are not met."

The room is silent while Duguay talks. He sounds like a professor giving a lecture. Lenny's stomach knots. To him, it's obvious this shit is too well rehearsed.

Over at the podium, Marshall looks nervous, not because of what Duguay says—he likes what he's saying; this is where he wants the meeting to go—but because of how Duguay talks. The nutty garbageman is a strange combination of intelligence and brutality that puts Marshall ill at ease. He's not the only one. Just about the entire room is scared shitless of Duguay.

Duguay finishes: "I'm guessing the executive wants to call off the strike, or at least extend our strike deadline, because not enough of us voted. Am I in the ballpark, Brother Marshall?"

Marshall looks flustered. Then he composes himself and says with his signature lisp: "You're more than in the ballpark, Brother Duguay. You've described the situation perfectly. We need to step back. We need to take more time, because we did not go about this in the right way the first time around…"

This brings Lenny to his feet. He's heard enough. "This is bullshit, Larry, and you know it!"

A few voices call out support for Lenny. He goes on: "You've got cold feet because you're not ready to lead us out on strike, so you're stalling. That vote was legit. I was there. I voted. I want the leadership to respect the mandate that was given. We got forty-eight hours! We gotta stand together and walk. Force the fuckers at City Hall to keep our jobs!"

Lenny gets some applause and whoops of support. Marshall holds up his hands to quiet the masses. He says, "Brother Lazaruscu, you used one correct word: *respect*. But what we need to respect are the bylaws of this Local. We can't go running around breaking our own rules. Where would we be then? We'd have as much credibility as management at City Hall that doesn't want to respect our collective agreement."

Lenny snaps, "What fucking collective agreement, Larry? It fuckin' expired months ago and your negotiating team has left us in the lurch ever since!"

Now it's Duguay's turn to enter the fracas. "Brother Lazaruscu, the president has spoken. Maybe you oughta learn something about respect. Both for your leadership and for the rules of this here union. You don't like it, maybe you should fuckin' leave!"

This brings thunderous noise from Duguay's gang of thieves. Lenny tries to rebut but the noise and tumult is too much. Marshall stands at the front of the room, holding back a grin. He does nothing to quiet the crowd. Finally, he speaks into the mic:

"Rules is rules. Numbers is numbers. We broke bylaw 43.2 by having only fifty-two per cent of the membership vote the first time around. We've got no choice but to call another vote. I suggest we give ourselves plenty of time to make the right decision. I say we call another vote for three weeks from now, at our next regularly-scheduled meeting…Can I have a motion to that effect?"

Immediately two-dozen hands fly up.

"Right, thank you, Brother Lewis. Let the minutes show we will vote in three weeks to determine if action is necessary to force an agreement. Can I have a seconder?" Marshall asks.

Another sea of hands.

"Let the minutes show Brother Wozniewski seconded the motion."

This just about kills Lenny. He glares across the room at Wally. The dumb stump looks stoned on Duguay's best B.C. bud. Cheeky fucker seconding a motion to delay the strike; it's too much for Lenny. He knows when he's beat. Just as Marshall calls for a vote on the motion from the floor, Lenny skulks out of the meeting room. He does not want to be there while a room full of lemmings follow Duguay over the edge of a cliff.

...

I've been fucked over and betrayed by my own union. It's supposed to represent me. I was a fool not seeing this coming, thinking the leadership actually had the balls to stand up and fight. I should have known Duguay would get to Marshall. That greasy politician spins whatever way the wind blows. Duguay has succeeded, or so it seems. He's cracked the leadership and stopped the strike and now it looks like he has support. I know there are still lots of guys out there who see past his bullshit and intimidation tactics. These guys know what's coming if we don't protect our jobs. But I know Duguay will shepherd every one of his fucking lambs out to the vote. He'll scour the membership to make sure everyone who can vote does vote. Over the next three weeks he'll be on the campaign trail spreading his bullshit around, coercing some guys, pampering others. Minds will change. He'll get to lots of the imbeciles and get them on his side. But not everyone can be bought for some coke and a blow job, can they? Not everyone is as shallow and weak as Wally Wozniewski, are they? There must be enough of the old guard still standing that Duguay won't sway enough to win. This is what I have to find out; this is what I'm up against. It's clear Marshall is nowhere on this. His strategy is to cling to power, to delay and ride emotion whichever direction it leads. What a gutless cocksucker. Just like every politician. I can't believe it, or maybe I do. This fucking job and all the bullshit that comes with it never ceases to amaze me. I need a drink, or six.

• • •

Back on the job Friday morning, Lenny climbs into the truck cab. Anton and Wally snicker like a couple of goofy kids.

"What the fuck's so funny, assholes?"

Wally says, "Hey, relax dude. Don't be so fuckin' tense. It's Friday after all."

It takes Lenny all of two seconds to realize they are both

roasted in the sun. He shakes his head in disgust and starts the truck. He pulls out of the yard, staring straight ahead through the windshield, trying to ignore Anton and Wally.

Lenny starts in hard at the first job site, riding Anton and Wally like a pair of mules. He barks orders, inspects their work closely, makes them do shit over. No dog fucking today, even though it's Friday. Anton and Wally wilt under the pressure. Their B.C. bud buzz fades to zilch. They bitch and moan, but Lenny hears none of it. By lunchtime they have spread as much KP as they usually do in an entire day. Lenny heads back to the yard for more.

When they get to the Barton Street District #2 yard, Anton and Wally think they're getting a reprieve to eat. Lenny snaps, "No, no. You two fuckers are gonna fill up the hopper with fresh KP. The day's only half over." Then he backs the truck up to a pile of crusty, old bitumen.

Anton protests, "What the fuck is all this about, Len? I know you're pissed about the meetin' last night but what the fuck?"

Wally is about to add to the complaint, but Lenny's dagger stare stops him.

Lenny goes, "Listen, you dumb fuckwads, I'm trying to prove a point here. This has nothing to do with being pissed about last night. This is all about showing you fuckbuckets what life will be like around here if we don't stand up to management and get a deal done, whether by honest negotiations or a fuckin' strike!"

Anton and Wally look stunned as usual.

Lenny goes on: "Let me explain it in words you can under-stand. We don't get a good deal with the city this time around, this cushy job of yours will change big time. You can say goodbye to the dog fucking. You can kiss goodbye the Fridays of doing fuck all, being baked on weed, and fucking off early to Hanrahan's to worship pussy. Get it: no more beer, dope, and cunt; at least not while you're on the job. And maybe even after the job. You'll be so fuckin' tired you won't be able to party."

Lenny's words start to register with Anton and Wally. In their small brains they try to imagine a job without beer, weed, and pussy. It's a bleak landscape that scares them.

Anton offers, "How d'you mean, Len?"

"I tried to tell you guys before. There will be cutbacks and they'll farm out our jobs to private operators. It will be nothing like it is now. You, Wally." Lenny points a large finger straight at him. "As a junior man, you'll be lucky if you even get to stick around the city. You'll most likely be out on your ass looking for a job delivering fuckin' pizzas for minimum wage or some such shit. Both you guys better fuckin' knock off all the dope smoking and give some thought to what's going on around here. You follow any of this?"

Anton and Wally look like scolded kids. Lenny's words start to filter through to what's left of their brains. Eventually, Anton speaks, "What d'ya think we should do then, Len? I mean, I don't wanna, like, lose my job and I don't want this job to change. I couldn't fuckin' take it if I had to stay straight and just work all day. That'd fuckin' bite big time."

Anton looks over at Wally but Wally doesn't look like he's so sure. Lenny says to Wally, "You thinking about Duguay, son? That what's eating you? You remember what I said about him and how he owns you? Yeah, I'd be worried if was you."

Wally squirms in his seat like he's got a bug up his ass.

Lenny goes on: "Seems you got two choices. You can stick with Duguay or watch your job go down the shitter. Tough call. Glad I'm not in your shoes."

Wally scratches his neck and readjusts his ball cap. He doesn't say anything. He just grunts and climbs out of the truck. Then he shouts back at Lenny: "Back the fuckin' truck up all the way so we's can get this KP loaded before dinner."

Lenny looks over at Anton still seated in the cab. "Seems your buddy there don't wanna talk about the strike right now. You might wanna try talking some sense into him. But before that, help that dog fucker load KP."

Anton slides out of the cab and grabs a shovel. Lenny watches the two of them in his side mirror. Anton and Wally dig their shovels into the cold, hard KP, barely budging it. Lenny grins at the sight of them struggling and then pushes the clutch in, setting the truck rolling backward.

• • •

Over on garbage, Duguay runs a more aggressive campaign. Helped by his biker buddies, he is flush with drugs. He passes the shit out like it's Halloween and everyone coming to his door is dressed like a grubby city worker. He's got something for everyone: weed for the potheads; speed for the maniac runners; a little crank for those who like to get cranked; heroin for a select few old-school dopers; Oxy and meth for the younger generation of reprobate garbagemen. The entire yard is hopped up on something. And they wash it all down with beer and whisky supplied by Duguay himself. All he asks in return is that they step up and uncloud their minds long enough on the evening of the last Thursday of the month to mark a big black X beside the NO option when the strike vote is called.

Duguay is confident he will have the full support of the yard. But things don't always go as planned. He runs into some resistance. Some of the old-timers don't appreciate his strong-arm tactics. They're insulted by his drugs-for-votes approach. Hell, some of the old-timers actually have a conscience and an opinion on the logjammed contract negotiations.

Duguay has trouble when he tries to hit up a crew of vets. Tommy Tindale is a grizzled thirty-year garbageman who loves his booze—of that there is no doubt. But when Duguay offers him a new bottle of Jack, Tommy refuses.

"What the fuck, Tindale? I know you love this shit. You and I shared a bottle a few times over the years. The fuck's up? You gone teetotaller all of a sudden?"

Tindale shuffles his steel-toed feet in the filthy garbage yard dirt. His truck-mates—Hank Petersen, the driver, and Tommy's co-runner/garbage thrower "Fast Feet" Freddy Barker—stand in solidarity with Tindale.

Duguay goes, "What about you two old drunks? You not up to it this morning? You gonna look this fuckin' gift horse in the mouth?"

Duguay proffers the bottle of Jack Daniel's to Petersen and Barker. They both start to tremble. Turning down a bottle of whisky, especially while at work, is not something either of them has ever done before. The three men have spent about seventy-five combined years on garbage. They would be hard-pressed to find a dozen days in all those years when they *didn't* have at least one drink on the job. That's how killer this job is. A man can work it the better part of his life and virtually never be able to face it sober. For Tindale, Petersen, and Barker to say no to free booze is a gargantuan step indeed. Sure enough, Tindale, Petersen, and Barker all decline the bottle. But Duguay doesn't press the matter. He's got other plans. Right when the three old-timers expect him to harass them, right when they're on the verge of maybe wilting and grabbing the bottle and making a beeline for their truck, Duguay turns away. "Suit yourselves, dog fuckers," is all he says. And then he shows them his back.

. . .

A funny thing happens the following Monday. Not funny ha-ha. More like funny fucked up.

Tindale, Petersen, and Barker are about halfway through their first run of the day. All three men are still feeling it, still drunk from the weekend, which is normal. Tindale stumbles a little, slurs his words, stinks of booze, and is sort of out of it. He's not the brightest bulb to begin with, mind you. So when Duguay shows up with his truck and tells Tindale to join him on the back for a special run to the North End to salvage copper pipe (something no garbageman can resist), Tindale doesn't register that this might be dangerous. Away they go. Duguay and Tindale are on the back of the truck. Jeff Smith, Duguay's regular driver, is up front.

A minute later, Smith pulls into a Horton's parking lot at the corner of Dundurn and King Street West, usual Monday work territory. Smith goes to the back of the truck and says, "Duguay, I'm gonna buy us a round of them Horton's breakfast sandwich specials. Feeling generous today. Why don't you drive a block or two with Tindale and clear a street before we go for the copper."

Duguay looks at Tindale. "This fine by you, Tommy?"

Tindale adjusts his ball cap and grunts. Then he says, "Yeah, sure, so long as we get the fuckin' copper and then I can gets back to my crew. I could use the extra coin after the weekend I just had."

Tindale laughs. Duguay and Smith nod and laugh along with him, putting the older man at ease.

Then Duguay says, "Sure thing, Tom. Hop on the back and we'll do Head Street while Jeff buys breakfast."

Smith vanishes. Duguay sidles in behind the wheel. He is not licensed to drive, but that hardly matters. He puts the truck in gear and pulls out onto King Street. Instead of turning north on Dundurn toward Head Street, Duguay speeds off into traffic, going west on King, over the 403, and then a quick right on Macklin Road. Tindale hangs off the back. Duguay gets the truck up to seventy kilometres per hour as they fly down Macklin, past the arena, into a desolate strip of road that ends by Cootes Paradise. There are no houses down this way. There is no copper pipe. Tindale is pretty sure he's not going to paradise.

Tindale sweats as he grips the handrail on the back of the truck that goes way faster than it should. At every small bump in the road Tindale is thrown into the air, his boots coming off the truck. He is airborne for a second before slapping back down on the foot-grips. Tindale peers to his right looking for help but all he sees is a contaminated creek full of carp and garbage that runs next to the 403 highway, where cars, trucks, and buses zoom past unaware of the runaway garbage truck.

"Fuck," Tindale says, suddenly slightly sober.

At the bottom of Macklin Road, Duguay hits the brakes hard and cuts the steering wheel left at the same time, causing the truck to fishtail. The force is too much for Tindale's gloved hands. He is sent rocketing through the air like he has been shot from a cannon. At the same time, Duguay jumps out of the cab of the truck. He runs after Tindale. For a second it seems like they're in a Bugs Bunny cartoon. Tommy flies through the air, features blurred, knowing he's about to hit an anvil or a cliff face, as if he is Wile E. Coyote and Duguay is the roadrunner. Instead, he hits a tree trunk. Tindale veers his head away at the last second and takes the full impact in his right shoulder, breaking bone, destroying his shoulder, dislocating his elbow instantly and jarring his entire body. His elbow is pretty much lost completely. His clavicle, humerus, radius, and ulna break and mash together in a heap. Bits of bone pierce the skin all the way down what remains of his arm. The rest of Tindale crumples to the earth broken. He is barely conscious. Blood spouts from his mouth and nose. Had he not averted his head at the last second, he would have broken his neck and died on impact. Duguay is beside him in a flash. He stands over Tindale for a second, making sure the older man is not dead. Then he raises his right work boot and steps down hard on Tommy's ruined left arm. Tindale screams.

"Good. You're awake. Hear this then. You shoulda played it smarter, you stupid old fuck."

Next Duguay kicks Tindale in the ribs with his steel-toed boots a few times. Blood so dark red it is almost black seeps out Tommy's nostrils. Then Duguay puts all his weight on Tindale's neck, standing on the downed man, coming as close to killing him as he can. Tindale sputters for breath. Blood, snot, and phlegm shoot in all directions. Finally, Duguay steps off him and kneels beside Tindale's bloody head.

"Change your mind yet?"

Then Duguay is back on his feet. He is hyper. Adrenaline speeds through his body, mingling manically with the drugs and alcohol. He takes out his cock and pisses all over Tindale. Shock starts to take over Tindale's body. Right at that moment, Duguay sweeps Tindale up and carries him to the truck like a load of garbage. Sure enough, he tosses him in the hopper. Tindale settles, nearly dead, into the shit-heap of garbage in the hopper while Duguay drives away, back up Macklin, east on Main, north on Dundurn to King Street, where Smith waits on the corner. Smith hops in the cab. Duguay jumps on the back and checks on Tindale. His body jostles around on top of garbage bags, broken boxes, an old lawn chair and some stray papers, all of it doused in the usual putrid seepage that runs into the hopper from the load in the back of the truck. The men call it garbage juice; fresh-squeezed by the truck blade that compacts tonnes of rotten rubbish.

Duguay is not sure Tindale is alive, but that hardly seems to matter. As Smith accelerates up Dundurn toward a sharp right on York Street, Duguay leans into the hopper. He grabs Tindale in one hand, holding onto the handrail on the side of the truck with the other. Using the momentum of the turning truck and his own brute strength, Duguay hauls Tindale—who weighs maybe 160 pounds soaking wet in the garbage juice—and tosses his body out of the hopper, away from the truck, across the median, into westbound traffic on York Street. Duguay watches it all. Tindale is again airborne until his filthy body hits the asphalt on York, making a horrible wet-sounding thud, before skidding to a stop on a broken line separating two lanes of traffic. There, an suv the size of a triceratops crushes Tindale. The man is unconscious at this point, of course, but his mashed face is somehow angled right at Duguay. For a second it's like their eyes meet. There is no love between them. In fact, Duguay laughs as he watches Tindale's head bounce off the asphalt between the front and back wheels of the suv. Then Tindale's body sort of somersaults like a pulpy ragdoll. There is blood all over the pavement, a new set of wounds all over his body, new broken bones and damaged organs to add to his woe. The suv stops. A small chain reaction is set off as cars behind the suv veer to avoid the accident. A small import driven by an old woman drives over Tindale's right foot, destroying his ankle and most of the bones in his foot, save for his toes that are protected by the steel plate inserted at the front of the boot. And then finally the action is over. Tindale lies motionless. Drivers jump from cars to check on him. Duguay plays along and runs over to the downed man. Smith, too, plays his part, radioing the main yard to report the accident.

By the time they are done with him at the McMaster Medical Centre, Tindale is strapped into a bed in intensive care with dozens of broken bones, vital organs punctured and compromised, a million tubes and wires coming out of what's left of him.

The city investigates. The Ministry of Labour investigates. The union investigates. Their conclusions are the same: a horrible accident, with the worker's high alcohol levels a contributing factor, a likely reason why he lost his balance and grip on the back of the truck and was thrown into oncoming traffic. Outcome: unsafe behaviour on behalf of the individual worker. Duguay and Smith corroborate the story. Marshall visits Tindale in hospital. The newspapers, radio, and TV report on the accident, with none linking the brutal incident to the possible strike. Lenny, of course, and many of the men, know exactly what went down. They know Tindale had no business running with Duguay's crew. They know Duguay fucked Tindale over to send a message to the rest of the membership to expect the same or similar if Duguay doesn't get his way.

• • •

Lenny needs a break. He goes out one night. He doesn't do it often. He prefers to drink at home alone. It's cheaper. He gets to sit and watch whatever he wants on TV. But tonight he feels the urge to step out away from the usual crap.

Lenny walks south on Hughson Street to where it meets Barton. He looks left, to the east. Hanrahan's is down that way a couple blocks. Beyond that, by another two blocks, is the District #2 yard. There is a good chance some boys from the yard are at Hanrahan's in pervert's row taking in the ballet. There is an even better chance that Duguay is there pimping peelers and arranging blow jobs in exchange for support against the strike. Lenny wants no part of that. He's out to forget city bullshit, not get his nose pressed into it. He especially wants to forget the shit that went down with Tindale. So Lenny turns right on Barton and heads toward James Street. There he walks south again, toward the city's old, dilapidated downtown core.

There is something weird about James Street North. There are people out and about, and not just the usual old Portuguese coots shambling to their clubs to play cards. And not just the odd crackhead whore either, wandering in a stupor. And not the Italian widows in their long black veils and black cardigans on top of black frocks over black shoes. Lenny notices there is a different sort of creature out that is not native to James Street North: faggoty hipster types and skinny high school girls who definitely don't go to John A.

"What the fuck?" Lenny mutters to himself. "Where did these tourists come from? This shit-dump street is suddenly trendy?"

It's been a long time since Lenny has walked up this way. He takes in the storefronts converted to art galleries.

"What happened to the tailor shops, fish markets, and laundromats?" he says.

There is a swank-looking pub called the Cock and Pheasant at the next corner.

"What the fuck? There's a place called the Cock and Pheasant in this neighbourhood? Cock and Pussy more like." Lenny laughs at his own joke. He feels better already, slightly buoyant.

Next Lenny sees a familiar landmark: the Armoury. From across the street he watches the Sea Cadets inside march around. Lenny's sure they're mostly North End kids. Back when he was eight or nine his mom threw him into the Sea Cadets. The North End has been feeding the Canadian military for generations. Working-class kids looking for steady jobs end up in Pettawawa or Gagetown. They wind up as foot soldiers living just above the poverty line in shitkicker towns, ready to die for their country when the call comes. Lenny snorts and shakes his head. He says to himself, "If the army was made up of rich folks, we'd be at peace forever." Lenny feels less buoyant.

Thirsty now, Lenny steps into an old-man bar called the Waldorf Tavern. Right away Lenny sees it has changed. There are big-screen TVs all over the walls. Music plays. The dartboards are still there, and the pool table, but the clientele is different. There are more hipster tourists that Lenny is sure come from the West End, Dundas, and Ancaster. They must be slumming in the city centre, like they're some kind of new bohemians. He scoffs and goes to the bar and orders a bottle of Export. Lenny drinks it down fast, leaning on the bar. The pain goes away. He orders another, with a shot of rye. He slugs back the rye and then downs the beer right after it. Lenny starts to warm in his sinuses, behind and under his eyes. He feels his shoulders free up and his knees relax. He has another rye and a beer to go with a pickled egg.

At a table to Lenny's left, kids fiddle with phones and devices. One skinny kid holds his phone up and pokes the display pad with soft, uncalloused fingers. He giggles and points at something on the screen. The other kids find it hilarious. They laugh and drink beer in colourfully labelled bottles.

"Definitely not native to the neighbourhood," Lenny says to himself.

Lenny looks around. He's not looking for a familiar face. He doesn't want company. He just wants to make sure the neighbourhood has not been completely taken over by young fucks with stupid phones and soft hands. To Lenny's relief, some neighbourhood crusties hang around the pool table. Lenny orders another beer and wanders over. He's never been much of a pool player. He only wants to watch, to get away from the kids, the TVs, and music.

A short, fat bald guy about forty and a tall scraggly guy around the same age shoot pool with a woman who looks to be early fifties, with dyed, dirty-blond hair. She's dressed like she's trying to look twenty years younger. Her jeans are too tight, with strategically placed, factory-formed rips and tears. Her too-small T-shirt has some kind of swirly design on the front over a purple and green Union Jack. She wears fuck-me boots. She is clearly drunk. The game is a bit of a mess. Balls scatter everywhere and from what Lenny can tell, the two guys aren't really trying to hit their shots. It's about prolonging the game and buying drinks for the cougar. She laughs and sputters incoherently. She scratches the white ball, nearly tearing the table's stained cloth cover. The two guys laugh at her. The bald guy steps up and knocks the balls around. Then he leans over and wraps an arm around the woman. He mashes his face in next to hers. They kiss, tongues out, lapping at each other like a couple of dogs. The scraggly guy doesn't want to miss out. He sort of leans into the woman's back and presses his groin into the ass of her tight jeans. Lenny can see where this is going. Anyone with half a brain can see where this is going. The three come apart. The woman tries to take another shot but loses her grip on her cue entirely. It skids away from her, sending a ball off the table rolling toward Lenny. He stops it with his foot. The woman looks over at Lenny through bleary eyes and cackles something. Her face contorts as she talks, lines tightening around her mouth and eyes where neither burgundy lipstick nor black eyeliner can conceal the ditches and valleys age and hard living have carved into her face. She is not a pretty woman, Lenny concludes. He stoops and retrieves the ball. He holds it in his palm, waiting for one of the pool players to come over to him but they don't.

The bald guy tosses his cue on the table and looks at his buddy. "Guess the game's fuckin' done then, eh Stevie?"

Stevie nods. He looks like he doesn't ever say much and just follows the bald guy's lead.

The woman stands on wobbly legs, listing like she is caught in a strong wind until the bald guy catches her, putting his hands on her hips. "Time to call it a night, love? Let's get some fresh air."

The woman can't speak. She can only sort of drool, causing her to wipe her mouth and smear her lipstick. She goes from unattractive to repulsive quickly, but the bald guy and Stevie don't care. Stevie grabs her purse off a table. It's a gaudy silver thing with stainless steel hoops and black leather straps, like it could be a bondage accessory. Held up by the bald guy, the woman shambles toward the front door and James Street while Stevie brings up the rear.

Lenny finishes his beer, plunks it on the bar and heads out after them. By the time he gets there they are gone. It's not that he planned to do anything to intervene or to turn it into a complete gangbang. It's just that he is drawn to the street to carry on somewhere. The cougar—whatever happens to her—has set her own course in life, Lenny concludes.

He moves further south on James Street, almost knocking over a bunch of kids who stand outside a bar smoking on the pavement. The place is a small bar sliced into the row of businesses. It's called The Brain Trust, which Lenny thinks is a stupid name for a bar. This seems to be the hub of the hipster shit, so Lenny decides to check it out. He wants to fuck with the hipsters, to put himself—a North-End native verging on becoming an old man; the type of guy who used to rule this street—right into their midst.

About six stools line up next to the bar. A few small tables are cluttered into the cramped space. Lenny looks to the back where The Brain Trust opens up a little. He sees kids drinking beer and red wine at a couple of ratty couches. Lenny decides on the bar. He looks at the taps and recognizes none of the names. He looks in the beer fridge behind the bar and it, too, looks foreign to him. A stocky bald guy comes over to Lenny. He's got dark brown eyes and a bit of a silly smile on his face, like he knows there is a certain amount of bullshit floating in the room but it's okay because the kids have money and money is what drives this world. Like Lenny, the guy is also older than the kids, also a bit out of his element. Lenny thinks this guy owns the place. He's a grade six teacher or a real estate agent or something and he owns the bar to top up his income and get some kicks taking money from idiot kids while sussing out the female talent at the same time. Smart fucker, Lenny thinks. But his scheming also reminds Lenny a little of Duguay.

"What can I get you?" the stocky dude says.

"Don't know. I want a beer but what the fuck is all this?" Lenny points at the taps.

The bald bartender knows whom he's dealing with. Locals come in here now and again.

"Try this." He hands Lenny an oversized bottle from the fridge. It's got one of those overly colourful labels on it, like what the kids were drinking at the Waldorf.

"Dead Elephant?" Lenny asks.

"It's strong. Strong like bull," the bartender says, and flexes his left biceps muscle.

Lenny slugs the beer and smiles. It tastes pretty good. It warms him behind the eyes.

"The first one's on the house," the bartender says. "I've never seen you in here before. Want to make you feel welcome."

Lenny is impressed but he also feels his stomach knot. The gesture summons up something about the bullshit with the city. Lenny nods a thanks to the bartender and drinks the beer.

By one A.M. Lenny has killed four Dead Elephants without getting off his perch at the bar. The bottles are set in a circle on the bar-top in front of him. Lenny didn't let the bartender take them away. He likes the colourfully labelled bottles and how, circled, it makes him think of the circus.

As a kid, Lenny went to a circus once at Maple Leaf Gardens in Toronto. He couldn't believe it. He was nine or ten years old. Lenny had only left Hamilton a couple of times before. He rarely even left the North End. His mom took Lenny and his sisters to the circus on the bus. When they got to Toronto, Lenny was spooked. The city was bigger. There were huge buildings. There were more people on the sidewalks, and everything moved faster. They walked from the bus station to the Gardens for the afternoon show. They sat way up high in grey seats, but Lenny didn't care. He could hear the roar of the lions. His view of the trapeze artists was clear. And he wasn't too close to the clowns, who disturbed him with their antics. It was the elephants Lenny remembers best. They wore colourful vests and had silly red hats strapped to their enormous heads. They walked so heavily that Lenny could feel the building shake, even way up where he was sitting. The entire thing was magic. Compared to the days of drudgery marching around in the Sea Cadets in the James Street Armoury, the circus was heaven. It was a pure escape like Lenny had never experienced before and seldom has since.

Staring at the bottles on the bar, Lenny stands, stamps his feet and makes a sound like an elephant, and then charges out of The Brain Trust back onto James Street North. There he piles into more of the smoking hipster kids, sending them toppling like bowling pins, as there is nothing to their slight and narrow bodies. Lenny laughs and blunders further south toward King and James, the old heart of the city.

Drunk, Lenny stops in at a shawarma place, even though he's not really sure what shawarma is. He steps inside and smells meat. That's good enough. He orders a beef shawarma wrap, sits by himself in the small shop and eats. Four East Indian kids sit at a table to his right. They are drunk. The two girls are under-dressed. One is fat. Her brown flesh gushes from her tight clothes. The other one is too thin, a rail of a girl in tight clothing that shows off her bones. The guys are dressed like pimps, Lenny thinks. They toy with phones and devices. They smell of money. They have come from some club where they threw their parents' money away.

Lenny thinks they will head home in cabs, snort cocaine and eventually fuck until the sun comes up. This makes Lenny feel lonely and maudlin. He does not finish his wrap. He leaves the greasy food on the table and walks out into the night. He sees more young, drunk kids. They are all kids to him, even though some are likely thirty years old. Lenny feels like a dead elephant by comparison. He leaves King and James and the downtown core, retreating home to Hughson Street. Outside his small house, Lenny vomits in the gutter. Then, alone, he shuffles into his home to sleep it off. The new day coming will only bring more bullshit.

• • •

Duguay also wants a night out, but not to avoid city politics. He's got campaigning on his mind. He needs to drum up support. He calls Smith.

"Pick me up in fifteen."

"Sure thing."

Duguay lives in a crappy bachelor flat in a small walk-up apartment building on Wentworth Street North, just south of Cannon Street. He doesn't drive. Doesn't have a valid licence; lost it years ago. Smith drives the truck at work and acts as Duguay's chauffeur after work. Duguay returns the favour the only way he knows, with free booze, drugs, and blow jobs from strippers. Smith is fine with the arrangement. Big surprise, that.

When Smith arrives, Duguay climbs into the passenger seat of Smith's 1983 black Monte Carlo. He's pimped it up. Oversized tires. Jacked up the back. Black leather interior. Baubles and shit decorate the dash. Pink panties hang off the rear-view mirror. When asked, or sometimes he offers the information on his own, Smith proudly says, "Yeah, peeled those off a ripper called Candy Cane at Hanny's myself. She said I could keep 'em. Never even fuckin' washed 'em since."

It's a source of amusement to Duguay. Whenever Smith drives him, he starts the trip by stuffing his nose in the underwear and giving the silky gitch a good sniff. He does it tonight, first thing.

"Pussy. Nothing fuckin' sweeter," Duguay says.

"You said it, brother."

Duguay glares at Smith. "Knock off the union talk, shit-brain."

Smith looks embarrassed. He tries to redeem himself. "Hanny's or the Pump?"

"Pump first. Gotta see a man about a horse."

Smith looks confused. "What the fuck?"

Duguay rolls his eyes, then spools a spliff and sparks it. Then he clarifies, "I gotta pick up some supplies, you fuckin' idiot."

Duguay is tense. He seldom has a harsh word for Smith. They've been drug buddies for years, since they both started on garbage nearly twenty years ago. The strike situation weighs heavily on Duguay. He's been hearing it from the Red Diamonds. The bikers are in a jam. Word is, the Rockheads from Quebec are threatening a turf war. The Diamonds cannot afford any sort of slowdown in their business or any fuck-ups with whom they influence. Duguay is their main man with the city. The bikers have guys in the steel plants, hospitals, hotels and service industry, among the maintenance staff at the university, and even a firefighter. They all sell the Diamonds' drugs directly to working men and women, to ease the pain and suffering that comes with working a shit job in a shithole city.

The Running Pump is a hard-assed bar on Wellington Street North. A few years back, the Diamonds had an old-time brawl in the Pump's parking lot with rival members of the Constantino family, a clan of thugs fronted by the vending machine business. The Diamonds took out Rocco and Marco Constantino but couldn't get to the patriarch, old man Dominic Constantino. Still, it was enough to give the bikers the upper hand they've held on the drug trade, until the latest challenge by the Rockheads.

Inside the Pump, Duguay and Smith go to a table in the back corner. They sit. Seconds later, a lithe waitress with suicide-blond hair puts bottles of Export in front of the garbagemen. Across the table, two Red Diamonds sit, somewhat slouched, lacking their usual lustre.

"Duguay. Smith," the one guy eventually says.

"Gentlemen," Duguay says, raising his bottle of beer in the air to pay his respects, before guzzling back the entire contents in one go.

This summons the waitress again. This time—feeling juiced and untouchable—Duguay puts a hand on her ass as she stands by the table. He grins a cocky grin. The bikers don't like it. It not that she's their property. It's Duguay's attitude that pisses them off. They come back to life. One of them stands.

"Quit fuckin' around, Duguay. You can wait to get your cock out later."

The waitress doesn't like the sounds of this at all. She scurries away.

Duguay feels their scorn. "Just havin' fun."

"Fuck that. Get your head back on shit that matters. We're here for business."

Next the biker draws out a tattered knapsack from under the table. It looks like it could contain a high school kid's shit, like books, smelly socks, scraps of paper, condoms and little drug baggies. Instead, it's jammed with an absolute cornucopia of drugs, plus a bottle of Jack Daniel's for Duguay. It's a buffet of mind-blasting substances. Everything a garbageman could want.

The biker holds the bag by a shoulder strap. He grimaces while he talks, "Your last freebie, Duguay. Either you get these fuckers to put down the strike or we might have to find us a new man to do the job." The biker looks at Smith.

Smith feels sorta proud for a second but then realizes his promotion might cost Duguay his life. Smith's not this hard core. He shrinks back and takes a hit of his beer.

"Understood," Duguay says.

Duguay takes the knapsack and gets up to leave all in one motion. Smith stands behind him.

The biker has one more thing on his mind. "On your way out, Duguay, be a gentleman and say you're fuckin' sorry to the lady."

Duguay can't believe what he hears. The Red Diamonds are truly jerking him around. His ass-grab hardly requires an apology. And it's the one thing that Duguay truly loathes: saying sorry to a woman. As far as he's concerned, it's the worst form of weakness, a mere rung above sucking dick or being a cop. The biker knows this. Their demand is about power. Who has it and who doesn't.

Duguay grips the knapsack and skulks out. At the bar he grunts an apology at the terrified waitress. She nods and slips away. The bikers laugh and taunt Duguay from across the room. The two garbagemen leave the Pump. Smith stays quiet. He knows better than to say anything as they climb into the Monte Carlo. Duguay is so pissed off and humiliated that he declines to sniff the panties.

Ten minutes later, Smith pulls into the parking lot behind Hanrahan's. Duguay comes back to life. He grabs the knapsack and opens the zipper. He pulls out a bottle of Jack Daniel's and has a hit. He passes it to Smith. Next he takes out a stash of cocaine, small servings in tiny plastic baggies wrapped in bigger plastic baggies. Like he is opening the layers of a Russian doll, Duguay digs down to the coke. Old-school, Duguay empties a dose of coke into the crook of skin between his thumb and first finger. He inhales it, then licks his crusty skin. Then he passes some coke to Smith, who does likewise. The men follow this with more Jack Daniel's. Fortified, they are ready for their meeting.

Inside Hanrahan's, about two dozen garbagemen and other city workers are assembled. This is Duguay's version of a meeting of the Local. But there will be no speakers, no one keeping minutes, no one checking who comes and goes to make sure they're union members. Duguay's gang of thieves knows its task. Portions of drugs will be divvied up among the men to pass around city yards with the strict reminder that for free drugs comes votes against the strike next Thursday. As well, the men will threaten violence and warn fellow city workers that their cars will be vandalized if they don't side against the strike. If there is resistance, Duguay tells his runners that they are free to mention Tindale's name. This should be enough of a warning to convince most.

Duguay's Hanrahan's meeting doesn't last long. The drugs are distributed like brown bag lunches. Then Duguay says, "Now get the fuck out and get to work. I wanna hang with my man Smith and sort out the rest of our fuckin' strategy."

The men disperse, disappointed. Clearly, most were expecting a full-blown party: Wozniewski, for example. Like Lenny predicted, Duguay owns Wozniewski and has brought him on to do his dirty work. Wally was clearly expecting a repeat of his night out a month back, but Duguay has a different form of business on his mind.

Smith looks confused again. "Why's everyone gotta leave?"

Duguay grips a bottle of Molson Export tightly in his right fist. He looks to the stage at the front of the club. A brunette is down on all fours on her stripping blanket for her first song. She is topless, but wears purple thong panties. Like a snake, she slithers across the stage using mostly stomach muscles, her fine, round ass coming up in the air. When she gets to the edge of the stage, she sort of pivots on her grey blanket and shows the crowd her ass. Duguay centres his gaze there and does not answer Smith's question right away. Smith looks at the stage too. He is likewise mesmerized by the ripper's fine form.

Finally, Duguay speaks. "I just wanna spend some time with my right-hand man. Know what I'm sayin'?"

Smith tenses. Duguay sounds serious. Like all the men, Smith was expecting a party. The Diamonds have clearly rattled Duguay.

Next Duguay leans across the table and grabs Smith by the scruff of his T-shirt. "You wanna meet her up close?"

This is more like it. Smith smiles crookedly. The two men stand and retreat through a door marked Staff Only. A bouncer takes note and follows the garbagemen. He meets up with Duguay and Smith.

"Can I help you boys with something?"

He knows their customer status.

Duguay calmly says, "The one on stage. She's new. Does she do private parties like some of the other sluts?"

The bouncer knows what he means.

"Yes, she does. I'll bring her here as soon as she's done her show."

Duguay grunts.

The bouncer continues. "I'll get some cocktails sent in in the meantime."

The word cocktails bothers Duguay. He puffs out his chest. "Fuck the cocktails, you faggot, and bring us a bottle of Jack Daniel's."

The bouncer takes offence. He is—of course—a very large man, bigger than Duguay by maybe twenty pounds. Smith senses the bouncer's anger and recoils. The big man could snap his neck like a chicken. Duguay, however, is not the least bit intimidated by the bouncer. He watches him and then takes more coke out of a baggie, sprinkles a line on a table, squats, and snorts. The entire time he keeps his eyes centred on the bouncer. Then Duguay returns to his full height. His head is like a pinball machine, firing off in all directions, fully alight. The bouncer backs away. He knows Duguay is tight with the Red Diamonds and he does not favour a watery grave in the harbour.

Two minutes later a blond appears with a bottle of Jack Daniel's.

Duguay says, "Close the door behind you."

She does as instructed.

Then he says, "Dance. That's what they pay you to do, isn't it?" He laughs. Smith joins in.

The woman begins a lethargic bump and grind routine in the small room. The two men drink whisky and watch. Duguay looks over at Smith every once in a while to check his reaction. Smith grins stupidly. Duguay sparks a joint, takes a quick hit and then passes it to Smith.

"Enjoy that one yourself, my friend. On me. Everything's on me tonight."

Smith does as instructed. He sucks back on the joint, watches the blond, and lets the marijuana buzz wash over him.

A couple minutes later the brunette from the stage comes in.

Duguay says, "Ah, here we go. Time to party right! The warm-up act is over. Time for the main event." He laughs loudly. The blond looks at him imploringly. "Yeah, you can fuckin' go. I never liked blonds much any which ways. Fuck off back outside to the regular fuckin' losers."

She slouches away.

Duguay is mad with a cocaine high. That, and the whisky and beer, has him feeling pit bull aggressive.

"What's your name, sweetheart?"

The stripper holds her grey blanket in front of her like a child. "Roxy May."

"Your mother named you good," Duguay says, snorting a

laugh. "I want you to entertain my man Smith here." He stabs a thumb in Smith's direction.

Smith is roasted out of his socks. The woman knows the situation. She was told when she got the gig that there are certain clients with certain connections that need to be "privately entertained." That entertainment includes sexual favours—blow jobs, mostly. It is a very thin line between stripping and prostitution, and many women cross it daily, stumbling back and forth in a drugged haze. OxyContin is Roxy May's drug of choice. In her profession, there is a strong need for pain relief.

Roxy May drops her blanket and steps in front of Smith. She wears only the purple thong panties. She puts her hands in her brown hair, twists and contorts her body and shimmies in front of the garbageman. Smith has been down this road many times with Duguay, but typically he has to wait for Duguay to have his fun first. It's not his birthday. He's not sure what's going on, why Duguay is being so generous. But it's not like him to question these things. Instead, Smith takes his cock out and strokes himself while Roxy May bends over and pulls her panties down, the thin wisp of fabric clinging momentarily in the cleft of her ass. She is a professional and knows what simpletons like Smith want. She is, however, wisely wary of Duguay, despite her opiated state.

"Turn," Smith says. Then he stands, his green work trousers falling to his ankles.

"Down."

Roxy May goes to her knees.

"Suck."

Roxy May takes Smith's cock in her mouth, while wrapping

her left fist around its base. She sucks and pumps at the same time, hoping to end things. Smith closes his eyes and leans back against a wall.

Duguay, meanwhile, has been watching all this unfold the way he knew it would. When he is sure Smith is seconds from shooting his load into the back of the ripper's mouth, he springs to his feet. Quickly, with one hand, he grabs Smith by the throat. With the other he grabs Roxy May by her brown hair. Smith gags and his eyes flash open. Roxy May gags as Smith's cock jostles, losing its rhythm in her mouth.

Duguay snarls, "You. Slut. Keep this fucker's cock in your gob."

Then he turns on Smith. "You. Fucker. Listen good."

He squeezes Smith's throat until the smaller man's face begins to purple. At the same time, Duguay jams Smith back against the wall. In other circumstances, Smith might be enjoying himself, might savour the blast of orgasm as his breathing is cut and oxygen is reduced to his brain, heightening his sexual experience. But Smith is pretty sure Duguay is not engaged in this sort of act. There is clear menace to his buddy's behaviour. Smith expels snot from his nose. He cannot nod his head to agree with Duguay. He can simply stare at him with bugged eyes. Roxy May, meanwhile, is also terrified. She keeps Smith's shrinking cock in her mouth and hopes her part in this will soon end.

"You want this blow job to be your last, you fuckin' Judas? You and me go way back, but don't for a fuckin' second think that means fuck all, Smith. I'll cut you down like I'd cut anyone down who fucks with me, got it?"

Duguay eases up on Smith's throat, and then takes his hand

away. Smith gasps and sputters and more snot shoots out of his nose. He tries to speak but no words come. Duguay doesn't want to hear it anyway. He continues his assault.

"I run drugs for the Red Diamonds! Not you, fucker! I don't know what you think you were doing there at the Pump but this is my fuckin' show. I own the city and you work for me, not the other fuckin' way around. It'll never be that way, so put that out of your fuckin' mind."

At this point Roxy May lets out a bit of snuffle. She still has Smith's withered prick in her mouth and clearly she's not sure what her role is any more. Duguay looks down at her. He snorts and then goes, "What's your fuckin' problem, bitch? You stay on your fuckin' knees 'til I tell you different."

For a second it looks like Duguay will hit her but then he changes his mind, redirects his rage back at Smith and cold cocks the other garbageman, sending him spilling into a stack of empty bottles in cardboard boxes in the corner of the small room. For good measure, Duguay springs over at Smith and kicks him while he's down, bloodying his face, rendering him semi-conscious. Then he steps back and stuffs his crotch in Roxy May's face. Frightened, she burbles and sputters some form of protest. They don't pay her enough for this shit. But Duguay is determined. He hoists his semi-stiff prick in her face and she takes it in her mouth. He skull-fucks her for a minute, then pulls back and spunks on her face and her tits. After he cums, he groans, and then looks over his shoulder at Smith lying on the floor.

"You stay in line, my friend, and maybe next time it'll be you getting your rocks off."

Next, from his pocket, Duguay draws out crushed Oxy tablets in a baggie. He drops it to the floor by the stripper's feet.

"A tip. For a blow job well done. And to keep your fuckin' mouth shut, unless it's my cock I want in there."

Duguay laughs and stomps out of the small room, back into the bar, and then out to the street. On Barton Street, he looks left and then right, his head blazing. He feels like he could fly or climb the side of a building like Spider-Man. He's not sure where to go, or what to do next, so he hoofs it away from the scene toward downtown.

...

Duguay's men fan out across the city, hitting every workplace where members of Local 689 are found. Free drugs are handed out in washrooms, lunchrooms, corridors, yards, workshops, storage sheds, inside the cabs of trucks, in parking lots, and even on the bus before and after shifts. But a funny thing happens. Some men and women want nothing to do with the drugs. They know what happened to Tindale, for example, and don't want a lunatic like Duguay calling the shots, even if it means putting themselves at risk. Others—and here's a point that Duguay truly overlooked— don't do drugs, plain and simple. Duguay has been in the garbage yard so long that he miscalculated that every city workplace is like his. That is, Duguay thinks that all city workers are party fiends who get through each and every day on the job with their brains cooked on some foreign substance. Turns out, this isn't the case. Duguay overlooked the fact many of the recent city hires come from new immigrant groups, folks who are trying to get their foot in the door in this country and who just don't touch any form of shit. Plus there are Bible-thumpers, teetotallers, neo-Conservatives, and old-timers who cling to the supposed virtues of the Protestant work ethic. These guys all turn their backs on Duguay's apostles when drugs are proffered. Then there are the guys who see it like Lenny. They fear what'll happen if the union wilts to management pressure. All of this resistance adds up to quite a few women and men who just won't be swayed by free drugs and threats of violence. Turns out, the world is a more decent and respectable place than Duguay surmised. Imagine that.

· · ·

Local 689 books the gymnasium at Bennetto Public School as a polling station for the strike vote. The vote goes down at the same time as a typical union meeting, from seven to nine P.M. on a Thursday night. The location and time work well for Duguay. Bennetto is in the heart of the city's North End and he figures that will keep some workers from the mountain and the city's outlying areas away. Duguay figures those dog fuckers are typically softer and more likely to avoid drugs and therefore not be on his side of the strike. The North End at night will keep some away, he thinks.

Marshall wants the strike vote to go off legit. He doesn't want any hijinks, no shenanigans, no bullshit. He's a fool for thinking this, of course. The process was corrupted a long time ago. Still, he has Signarsson and Lujic stand guard outside the school, to see that no brawls take place. Inside the school, a ballot booth is set up. Union staff support is provided from the provincial head-quarters, as an added layer of legitimacy. To the untrained eye, the operation looks genuine.

At 6:45 P.M., there's a queue of members waiting to vote, including Lenny and Duguay. They avoid each other. At this point, it's a standoff between them. The early high turnout bothers Duguay. He sees faces he doesn't recognize, including many young, sober faces. Lenny also notes that the miscreant population of city workers is well represented, such as Smith, Wozniewski, and other drug runners. Smith looks to have forgiven Duguay for nearly strangling him the other day while he was getting a perfectly fine blow job. He stands near Duguay, but not within arm's reach. Wozniewski looks stoned. Lenny can see this. He doesn't see Anton. Maybe he came to his senses and has separated himself from the hedonistic side of the Local. Like Duguay, Lenny also doesn't recognize a lot of the members. What's clear is that many are set to vote.

When the doors open, Duguay lets out a party howl. He's among the first into the school gym. Signarsson growls at him to take it easy but that has no effect. Duguay gets it over with quickly. Lenny is more tranquil and contemplative. He waits in line and then marks his X on the ballot in favour of the strike. Then, like he always does, he makes the lonely walk back to Hughson Street knowing there's nothing left for him to do.

Duguay, on the other hand, summons Smith after both men have voted.

"Let's go party."

Smith looks at him sideways.

"Fuck, will you get over that shit from the other night?"

Smith smiles weakly.

"I was just like sending you a message. I never planned to kill you or nothing. You think I'd do that?"

Smith doesn't look sure.

"Believe me, fucker; if I was gonna kill you, you'd fuckin' well know it. You'd fuckin' well know it because you'd be fuckin' dead, my friend."

Smith's weak smile goes away.

"Now go get the car."

Smith scurries away.

Inside the Monte Carlo, Duguay goes, "Here then," as he sniffs the pink panties, "Just like old fuckin' times!"

And away they go to Hanrahan's. This time, to make up for last week, Duguay lets Smith get a full and proper blow job from Roxy May—but not 'til he's had his cock sucked first, of course.

• • •

At work the next morning, Lenny is calm. Anton and Wally are still assigned to his truck. Lenny gets his job sheet from the fore-man after roll call just past seven A.M. and walks to the truck. Anton and Wally join him. Lenny doesn't have anything to say. Anton tries to coax him into talking about the strike but Lenny is not interested. He leads a typical day. The men do their work, just enough to look respectable. They fuck the dog a little, although Anton and Wally remain sober. The day passes as if all three men are in a holding pattern, waiting for the night to come.

...

Duguay is not calm over on garbage. He starts his morning slamming crystal meth in the cab of the truck while waiting for Smith to get them out on the street. The rest of the day, Duguay is manic, but he directs his rage toward the job. He runs the streets like a man half his age, tossing garbage like a machine. His running partner for the day is a new hire named Dmitri Kalatov, a big, evil-looking Russian.

Duguay snaps at one point, "You vote last night, Russian?"

Kalatov gives him an icy stare and then answers. "I'm on your side with this. I hate the fuckin' union."

Duguay smiles.

Kalatov finishes with, "The next time you refuel with meth, give me a blast so I can keep up with you."

This is the type of solidarity Duguay likes. And so his day goes; his drug crew runs two-and-a-half loads to the incinerator, hauling nearly nineteen tonnes of garbage off the city streets. It amounts to a good day's work.

When the day is done, Duguay grabs Smith by the arm. "Let's me and you go for a few drinks at the Pump before we head to the meeting. I want to be ready to hear the results of our fuckin' victory."

Smith, of course, doesn't argue.

...

The convention centre meeting room is packed to hear the results of the vote. Signarsson and Lujic check every woman and man in the room. They are all paid-in-full members of the Local. Marshall is beyond nervous. He shits bricks. He has never stood before the entire membership before. There are faces in the room he's never seen before and who have never seen him. It's standing room only.

Eventually, Marshall calls the room to order. He's got his big black dildo marker. He whacks it against the mic. Signarsson and Lujic help by waving their arms in the air and hollering for order. The crowd does not settle easily. Marshall looks around desperately, his leadership skills waning at the critical moment. This brings Duguay to his feet. More than to his feet: he marches right to the front of the room and hunches over the mic.

"Everyone sit the fuck down and shut the fuck up! Let's get this party started right!"

It works. The brothers and sisters settle into chairs. Others lean against the wall. More stand at the back by the barred doors.

Marshall steps to the mic. He lisps, "Brothers and sisters, thank you for coming out on a Friday night. I am pleased to say the vote yesterday went well. The turnout was incredible. Ninety-seven per cent of the membership voted. That's more than eight hundred of you. And I think there must be that many in the room now to hear the results. Clearly, you all care about one another…"

This is enough for some. "Cut the bullshit and give us the numbers, Larry!"

Marshall scrunches his shoulders and shuffles some paper on the speaker's podium. "Yes, the numbers. I'm getting to that. First, I want to thank the strike committee: Brothers Signarsson, Lujic and myself, along with Sister DiPietro, who verified the vote."

"Larry! The fucking numbers! Jerk yourselves off some other time and do it in private like the rest of us!"

Quick laughter from the crowd.

"Right. Well, here it is then. Like I said, we had over eight hundred votes cast. Eight hundred and twelve, to be exact, and the results are amazing…"

"Give it to us straight, Larry!"

Marshall clears his throat. He tries to cover his lisp, but it doesn't work. He speaks with less conviction than usual. "The raw numbers are four hundred and seven for a strike and four hundred and five against. It couldn't be any tighter."

This is not the decision Lenny, Duguay, or anyone was expecting, and no one is happy.

Duguay erupts to his feet and bellows: "Missed it by a fuckin' cunt hair! But that can't be right! How the fuck does it split right down the fuckin' middle?"

Lenny is next on his feet, "Brother Duguay, I don't often agree with you, but this outcome stinks! Larry, what's next?"

Others holler input. Marshall waves his arms and calls for order. Then he slowly walks over to a piece of flipchart paper and writes "LESS THEN 50 PER CENT." He stands and looks at it. Signarsson and Lujic join him, gazing at the grammatically-incorrect phrase. All three men shake their heads. Then they turn and go to the mic together. For Lenny, it's starting to look a little too well choreographed. But he waits to hear what comes next.

Marshall speaks: "Brothers and sisters, Brother Duguay—despite his inappropriate analogy—has it right. The results of the strike vote are too close. They must be looked at as inconclusive. This is less of a mandate to strike than we had the first time. And the first time not enough of you voted. This means we're split and can't act one way or the other. Right now, the leadership could vote." Here Marshall gestures at Signarsson, Lujic, and then points the dildo marker at himself. "But we'd still be pretty much dead even. Right now we need to stand alongside each other and clearly we're not doing that. I have no choice but to declare the vote a tie for all intents and purposes. We're simply no better off. Nothing is any clearer…"

The room goes absolutely quiet for five seconds while hundreds of men and women digest Marshall's words.

Then from the middle of the room someone hollers: "Impeach the president!"

This is followed by: "Peaches? What the fuck? Peaches?"

"IMPEACH! IMPEACH! Look it up, retard!"

Marshall leans across the speaker's podium toward Lujic. "What the fuck does impeach mean?"

The mic picks up Marshall's voice.

"It means toss the fuckin' president out the door onto his fat ass!" someone shouts.

"Eh?" Marshall mumbles.

Another voice screams: "Get rid of him! Get rid of the president now! He's not leading us anywhere!"

The crowd is on the verge of rioting.

Marshall tries to restore order. "Now, now, let's not be hasty." He waves his dildo marker around, but no one seems to care.

"Not be hasty? You've gotta be fucking kidding! You never do nothing quick or slow, you useless cocksucker of a useless president!"

A tomato flies through the air and splats against the wall behind Marshall. Lenny thinks it must the Italians or the Portuguese.

He recognizes a ripe, round, red tomato when he sees one. Not store-bought, no way. Another slices through the air and hits Lujic square in the forehead. He growls into the mic. "Who the fuck threw that?"

No one fesses up.

Instead someone hollers, "Can we really get rid of the president? Someone look it up! Who's got a copy of the fuckin' constitution on them?"

Marshall makes one last call for calm but it goes nowhere. It is clear to him he is a doomed man. But still he says into the mic, "Brothers and sisters, I urge you to stay calm. Respect the process. Respect the process. Respect…" his lisping voice trails off as tomatoes zoom over his head.

Then Petersen from garbage emerges from the crowd. He marches straight over to Marshall and grabs the black marker out of his hand. In his other hand he holds a palm-sized booklet. Petersen goes to the flipchart paper and writes "16.3." Then he steps over to the mic and asks, "Anyone know what that number means, brothers and sisters?"

Immediately, a voice calls out: "For God so loved the world, that he gave his only begotten Son, that whosoever believeth in him should not perish, but have everlasting life."

This creates momentary confusion. Then Petersen snarls, "That's 3:16, you Bible-thumping twat. I'm talking about 16.3. 16.3 from our constitution means the Local membership can call for a vote of non-confidence when the leadership shows no fuckin' leadership, when they act like a bunch of pussies."

Petersen pauses for a second and then says, "No disrespect to the sisters in the room."

"None taken, cocksucker," a sister shouts out, which gets the biggest laugh of the night.

Petersen snickers and then carries on, "A vote of non-confidence can happen any time when we have quorum when the situation calls for it. That's what section 16.3 says. It says so right here in black and fuckin' white!"

Petersen holds the Local's constitution up and waves it around. Now he does look like a preacher with a sacred text. Marshall, meanwhile, looks scared shitless. Signarsson and Lujic looked confused. So Marshall does the only thing he can think of: "Get that fucker away from the podium," he snaps at Signarsson and Lujic. The two big men grab Petersen and start dragging him away. Then the tomatoes really start flying, along with the occasional shoe and flipchart marker. Marshall realizes his recourse to violence is futile. Tomato-stained, he slouches to the podium and says, "If this is the will of the membership, then I won't stand in the way. I will respect the democratic process."

"What the fuck? Speak fuckin' English, Larry!" someone screams.

Marshall holds his arms up like Richard Nixon. "I am not a crook! I am not a crook! But I hereby resign my presidency and dissolve the entire executive!"

More hollering from the crowd: "Marshall's fuckin' lost it for good! There's your confidence vote. That lisping fucker is stepping down before we can throw him out! Gutless prick!"

The meeting has lurched from strike vote debate to election, all in a matter of minutes. It reminds Lenny of when the Berlin Wall came down, and spontaneous violence in Bucharest erupted when regular folks from the old country overthrew and then executed their leader all in a torrent of emotion. Lenny feels a similar swell of emotion when he sees Duguay storm to the front of the room to accept a nomination for president. Lewis, who has taken over chairing the meeting for some reason, then calls out: "Are there any other candidates for president of the Local to replace Marshall?"

Lewis scans the room. He is sure no one will come forward. He is stunned when a hand shoots up. A skinny guy who looks like Tindale says: "I nominate Brother Barker!"

Fast Feet Freddy Barker stands and drunkenly slurs, "I accept."

Lewis snarls. "Right then, we have two men wanting the job. Anyone else?"

Lenny turns to the man next him in the enormous hall. "I'll run if you nominate me."

The guy looks horrified. "No fuckin' way, brother. I don't want what came to Tindale."

"Pussy."

Lenny looks down the row of seated men. All turn their eyes away. But behind him, a sister he doesn't know says, "I'll nominate you. What the fuck. I don't want that animal Duguay in charge."

Lenny says, "You've got balls, sister."

She laughs and stabs her arm into the air. "I nominate the brother here." She points at Lenny.

Lenny shouts out, "I accept!"

Lewis's eyes bug out, but Duguay just laughs. He knows in a public forum like this that it will be no contest. Barker and Lenny go to the front of the room. The three candidates line up by the speaker's podium. Each speaks for a brief time into the mic. Barker babbles and is incoherent. Duguay is loud and bullying. Lenny tries to appeal to traditional trade union principles. Lewis calls for shows of hands for each man. First he points to Barker and bellows, "Up or down, brothers and sisters!" A dozen hands go up. Next it's Lenny. Here a greater portion of the room offers their support. Still, it's clear Duguay is poised to win. When Lewis calls out "Up or down" for Duguay, just about the entire room votes for him. Clearly, members vote more than once, fearing being seen not supporting the insane garbageman.

From the front of the room, Duguay roars: "Call me Mr. fuckin' President from now on!"

Lenny knows he has lost. The Local bursts into a party-like atmosphere. Marshall is out, the strike situation is no clearer, and Duguay is now officially in charge.

Amidst the chaos, Lenny shakes Duguay's hand. "Congratulations, Brother."

Duguay fires back, "Yeah, thanks. And by the way—fuck you, Lazaruscu!"

Lenny is not surprised. He skulks for the exit and leaves. Outside he stands on the pavement by the convention centre. Lenny looks skyward into the starless murk above the city. He talks to himself: "What the fuck just happened? This is a goddamned nightmare come to life."

Lenny shakes his head. Then he makes the lonely walk north on James Street, back to his small house on Hughson Street North.

...

Word of the fiasco at Local 689 reaches the provincial and national offices of the union quickly. A decision comes down that nullifies Duguay's usurpation of the presidency. The shit hits the media, further making Local 689 the butt of the Saturday editorials and commentary.

Union staff is assigned to take over completely. A provincial rep steps in to replace the servicing rep from the Hamilton union office who was leading the bargaining committee. The new rep gets her marching orders straight from National office. The main order: no more embarrassing and insane stunts from within Local 689. National suspends bargaining until the Local is back in control and has legitimate leadership. Meanwhile, the city revels in watching the Local implode. The city is happy to delay bargaining and extend the previous contract.

...

Even though he thinks he's president, Duguay still does what he always does and goes to the garbage yard Monday morning. He finds out his short term as president is over when he rolls in with Smith. Petersen stops Smith's car and summons Duguay out. Smith drives on, parking his car.

Petersen says, "Duguay, you're done as president."

Duguay barks, "What the fuck? Who says?"

He throws his cigarette to the ground and stamps it out with his right work boot.

"National office stepped in and declared the position vacant over the weekend."

"Those fuckers can do that?"

"Looks like it."

"And the strike?"

"It ain't gonna happen. You won that fuckin' battle, Duguay."

Duguay smiles, then blurts, "Fuckin' right!" He looks at Smith coming from his car. "You hear? No fuckin' strike after all."

Smith slaps Duguay on the back. "Well done, *Brother*."

Duguay growls.

Then Duguay goes to Petersen, "I didn't want to be fuckin' president anyway. Only a cocksucker would take that job. What's gonna happen to Marshall and those other losers, Signarsson and Lujic?"

"Back to the rank and file. Back to their regular jobs, as far I can tell," Petersen says.

"Well, then that's fuckin' something. Make those pricks work for a living for a change. But who's in charge of the Local?"

"National, I guess. Until we have a real election."

"Fuck sakes."

"Yeah."

Duguay pushes past Petersen into the yard's garage. The men mill about, afraid of what to say. But Duguay is gregarious. He beams and struts around. The mood lightens. The tension is gone. Duguay shouts out, "You fuckers hear? No strike. I'm open for business as fuckin' usual."

Smith gives a party howl.

Then Kerwin, a foreman, comes over to Duguay. "My office."

Duguay wants to refuse at first. But then he follows. The foreman closes the door to his office.

"Sit, Duguay."

Duguay pulls out a chair, spins it around and sits on it backward, draping himself over the back. His mood is still buoyant. There is nothing Kerwin can say that will kill it. The strike has died, or is as close to death as possible. Business will carry on, no matter what his knucklehead foreman has to say.

"I got a call last night from the director of public works," Kerwin says.

Duguay just looks at him, not sure where this is going.

"You remember ten years ago or so you put in for a foreman's job?"

Duguay doesn't remember. He says nothing.

"Well, it seems you're being offered a job as a floating foreman over at District 2."

Duguay narrows his gaze. "What the fuck?"

"You heard me right. The director needs you at District 2, if you want the job."

Duguay snorts. He's been a garbage man nearly twenty years. He gave up on getting out of throwing garbage years ago, despite putting in for the foreman's position. He stands. "When?"

"As soon as possible. Like today. Looks like your days tossing garbage are over. Welcome to management, if you take it."

Kerwin stands and offers his hand.

Duguay looks at the hand. He doesn't shake it. Instead he says, "Gimme a fuckin' second."

He leaves the office and walks out to the yard where trucks idle. He looks over at his truck where Smith sits with Kalatov, waiting for him. Other trucks roll out of the yard to start their Monday runs. It's hot. The humid air is mixed with the stench of diesel fumes and garbage. Duguay holds his left hand up in the air and signals to Smith. He calls out, "Hold on for a fuckin' second." Then he flips open a cell phone and calls another cell phone number. After a couple rings, the Red Diamond picks up.

"Better be fuckin' important, Duguay, you bastard."

"This qualifies."

"Yeah?"

"Yeah. Get this. The city suddenly wants to promote me to foreman. I sunk that strike and now they want to reel me in. I think I should take it, like we talked about years ago. It'd be good for business, no?"

"Foreman fuckin' Duguay. You a leader of men, eh?"

"That's what they're offering."

"Don't be a fuckin' idiot, then. Take it. You'll be tighter with pricks that make more money. We can double our sales. You sell to the foremen and any other management you can. We'll move Smith up to work the lowlifes."

Duguay looks across the yard at Smith. For a moment, a human emotion washes over him, and he feels proud Smith will get his chance after years of licking Duguay's boots and taking his seconds at Hanrahan's.

"Sounds like a fuckin' beautiful plan."

Duguay clicks his phone shut.

Twenty minutes later he steps out of a city foreman's pickup truck at the District 2 yard.

...

When Lenny comes back into the yard for dinner, Duguay waits for him, leaning in the threshold of his new office. Lenny thinks he's not seeing things right. Duguay helps him out: "That's right. I'm a fuckin' white hat now. Right here in your face, Lazaruscu."

Lenny can't believe it. Insult to injury just doesn't cover it. It's more evidence the world is a fucked up, unjust place.

Lenny goes to step around Duguay. He wants nothing more than to go to the lunchroom to eat in relative peace.

Duguay blocks his way. He breathes into Lenny's face. He smiles, his handlebar moustache peaking up at the corners of his mouth. Then he says, "I'm in charge of men. Can you fuckin' believe it, Lazaruscu? That union shit is small potatoes compared to this. That's yesterday's fuckin' news, my friend."

Lenny just shakes his head in disbelief.

"Believe it. Even if you don't want to. Wrap your fuckin' melon around it. I'm in charge of you. I own your fuckin' ass. I run this circus officially now."

"Circus?" Lenny asks.

Duguay snorts.

Other men push into the District 2 building. They eyeball Duguay suspiciously and then move on to the lunchroom. Lenny wants to join them, to step away from this bullshit, but Duguay puts a hand on his shoulder, stopping him. "What I say goes. I can fuck you around as much as I want and no one can stop me."

Lenny fires back, "The Local might have something to say about that. You're out as a member now. You know that, don't you?"

"Fuck the union. What's it ever done for me?"

There's that line again, one Lenny has heard too many times. "It kept you in a job, Duguay."

"The fuck it did, Lazaruscu. It was my brothers of a different kind that kept me in that job. How bad is your memory? The union just got in my fuckin' way. But no more. I'm a fuckin' foreman now. That gig on garbage served me well, but I'm on the other side now, this side. The side that fucks you over."

Duguay smiles and steps aside. "Better get your dinner in while you can, dog fucker." He laughs and struts into his new office.

Lenny heads for the lunchroom, even though he's not hungry anymore.

• • •

I put in for a foreman's job once. That was about seven years ago. I even interviewed for it. But something told me—a gut feeling during the interview—that I'd never get the job. There was something patronizing and false about the process, like they had their man and interviewing me was a charade. A junior man got it, a guy who came out of nowhere.

A few other men I worked with got interviews and all of them had a feeling that the deck was stacked from the start. Some guys kept trying, putting their names in for every posting that came up. They were desperate to get off the job. Foreman's positions were the only out, as far as they were concerned. They were wrong. Those jobs were carrots they would never grasp. Those positions are reserved for a select few. It didn't matter how qualified you

were, how well you did on the interview. Christ, you could probably suck a few cocks and it still wouldn't get you the job. I gave
up. I knew KP driver and lead hand was as high as I was ever going
to get.

When I hit twenty years of service, I just told myself I was on
the downside, heading toward retirement way off in the distance. I
looked at it this way: the job was like one big, drawn-out workday
and I was into the afternoon. All I had to do was ride it out for
another twenty years, call it a day, and then survive on a pension.
Along the way, I'd stay sane with a reasonable amount of dog fucking, while hoping to keep the bullshit to a minimum. Duguay as
my boss might just be too much bullshit to endure.

· · ·

The lunchroom isn't crowded. Only half the crews have come in
for dinner. The Italians from the cement crew are here, of course.
They never eat out. Their dinner ritual is steady and predictable.
They each start by laying out individual cloth napkins on the
lunchroom tables. And then they slowly open lunch buckets and
draw out unbuttered bread, cheese, salami, tomatoes and pep-
pers. Each guy has a paring knife. They meticulously assemble
their lunches on the napkins and then eat slowly and deliberately.
When they're done, they play cards until twenty to one. No one
outside their crew ever joins them.

The asphalt guys are here, too. They're a more ragtag group;
a blend of brown bag lunches and takeout food. They talk while
they eat and don't play cards. When they're done, some guys move

on to their cell phones and mobile devices or the *Toronto Sun*. Others head out to the yard for a butt.

The weed crew don't even sit together. They're scattered around the lunchroom. They know they are the vermin of the yard, the lowest of the low. They're embarrassed to be seen together. Some of those fools don't even eat. They forget their lunches or are too broke to afford food, spending all their money on booze, dope, and peelers. They don't have cell phones and I doubt any of them can read, so there are no newspapers among them.

The two yardmen—Henderson and Oflanski—sit together; eating, nodding, gesturing, and snickering. They're both certifiably insane.

My crew—Anton and Wally—sit over in the corner, by the vending machines that were put in last year. Wally guzzles Coke and eats a bag of barbecue chips. Anton at least has a lunch bucket. He mows down on what looks like a cheese and cucumber sandwich. I stand frozen a pace or two inside the lunchroom. For some reason, I can't go any further.

Anton eventually notices me and calls out, "Lenny, come and eat."

I've been pushing the men all day, and they saw Duguay busting my balls, but still Anton wants me to sit and act normal. I can't. I don't answer him. He says something else but his words sound rounded at their edges, mottled and indecipherable. I don't want to hear any words. It's Monday dinner. There is a long workweek ahead. There are months yet before this year even ends. And then a whole stack of years before I will ever truly relax.

Anton gestures to me, beckons me to sit. I don't hear him at all now. His head looks like an elephant's. Wally's too. I see grey, grizzled skin, and long trunks on their faces. I look around the room. All the men look like elephants. I stand in the centre of the room. I feel like I'm back at the circus, under the big top, rather than Maple Leaf Gardens. This place feels like a three-ring circus. Look at all the elephants. Am I the ringmaster? Can I tame elephants? Perform tricks and amazing feats of bravery? Am I dressed in a tuxedo, wearing a silly little red hat, standing on the back of a shuffling elephant? Sometimes it feels like it, but, still, it can't be. I'm a dog fucker, nothing more.

I walk slowly past Anton and Wally and find an empty, quiet table. I sit alone. I open my lunch bucket and reach for a hard-boiled egg. I peel it and start eating. It's my dinnertime. I'm in no rush. I'll take my sweet time. Fuck Duguay. Fuck everyone in this room. Fuck the Local. Fuck this job. I'll go back to work when I'm ready.

MATTHEW FIRTH was born and raised in Hamilton, Ontario. He now lives in Ottawa where he works by day for a national trade union. He is the author of three earlier collections of short fiction, most recently *Suburban Pornography and Other Stories* (Anvil Press, 2006). Paris' 13e Note Editions will publish a collection of his fiction in French translation titled *Sur Le Cul* in 2012. He is co-editor and publisher of the litmag *Front&Centre* and has run the micro-press Black Bile Press since 1993.